THE CANNONS OF MERRYLAND

First edition. March 12, 2023.

ISBN: 979-8215324332

Written by Daniel Sokoloff.

The Cannons of Merryland

A novel by

Daniel Sokoloff

Also by Daniel Sokoloff
Dream of the Ash: A Book of Mystical Poetry
The Struggle: A Novel of Demon Land

A note on the text

This story, and all stories of Demon Land, take place on a planet called Erde. They do not speak English, French, Hebrew, or any modern, earthly human language there, so artistic liberties have been taken on the words, names, and entities invoked and used by the characters described in these stories. While many of the roots and names might not translate perfectly, it should be noted that many of the angels, original demons (the ones that live in Hell), and deities are the same ones we know in the grimoires we have in our own occult traditions. Erde is not a fictional, mythical planet in another dimension. What its relationship to our own time period, world, or lives isn't clear to this writer yet, but should become apparent in due time. Until then, Ave Satanas!

Chapter 1: In the Trenches

Marcus stood by the heavily fortified glass of the tiny window, one of only three in the War Room. As a rule, there were not many windows in Fort Sunstrike, but there were a few small round ones, placed to give a quick glance at the battlefield below. Most recon was done by technicians at the telescope bays, which were built into the fortified walls. More intelligence was gathered from the cannon stations around the battlefield, which were connected to the fort via a network of underground tunnels. The hiss of distant HellsBreath blasters and the rattling of machine guns did not draw his attention any more than the occasional roar of a cannon, firing its explosive payload at a distant target. Marcus was eyeing the gloomy sky wistfully, imagining how the cold air would feel on his skin, under his

massive black wings.

Like the wings of a giant eagle, his wingspan was nearly twelve feet long, and could carry him higher than any aircraft in the Meridial Air Force. They were folded against his back at present, and were too huge for him to ever hide, but he had no reason to do so. Here in Fort Sunstrike, he was the final weapon in their arsenal, the single strongest missile they could use against their demonic enemy. His heart ached to be set loose, free to fly through the sky again.

Even in that direction though, the war was present. The enemy's spiked flying saucers hovered in the sky, circling the battlefield's perimeter, seeking for the right route to reach Fort Sunstrike. The demons had learned the hard way that their cannon-fields were not to be underestimated. Capable of hitting targets on the ground and thousands of feet in the air, the cannons had laid the tremendous metal snakes and flying machines of the enemy to waste, and shattered countless squadrons of their Ghoul Troopers and Locusts, littering the hills with their corpses and guts of their war machines.

"Let them throw everything they have at us, it doesn't matter. Their desperation will just expedite their failure in taking Merryland. With any luck, they'll be running back to Demon Land with their tails between their legs within the month," General Dobbs was saying to President Jerome Novak. The president was a small nervous man, with spectacles that he was obliged to push back up on his nose whenever they began to slide down his long nose.

"But I'm telling you, they found out somehow that I'm here, that's why they keep sending more and more hardware to the edge," President Novak insisted.

"That's utterly impossible," General Dobbs said, stroking his handlebar mustache pridefully. "No one has left this fortress except to fortify the cannons since the siege began two months ago, and you know none of our forces knew you were holing up here because you came here disguised as one of my bodyguards. The enemy still thinks you're squirreled away at the Dragon's Keep."

"But Gunn, tell him what you were just telling me before Dobbs came in," President Novak said.

Marcus turned to face the three men, standing around their Astitution Table. It projected a holographic model of the battlefield, with Fort Sunstrike on its high hill in the near center. All around was a vast sea of hills like green and grey waves, each with a huge cannon installed on them. The barrels on some swiveled around and around, tracking their targets, while others were stationary, waiting for something to blow apart. The teams for the cannons were based below the ground, situated in their stations inside the hills. Their telescopes roved far and wide, peeking out at their enemies, and the explosives that were installed in each and every cannonball were manufactured right there, beneath every cannon, ready to be loaded immediately after the last was fired. To bolster the formidable threat of the cannons, snipers were hidden amongst the hills, hiding under camouflage sheets as they picked off any demons foolish enough to poke their heads out of their trenches. The snipers were colored red on the Astitution Table, and the cannons were blue.

"It's true, Dobbs, they've been stepping up the reinforcements to this site, but I really don't think it will ever be enough. They know we don't have many forces here, and they think that they can take this fort easily enough if they can just break through our cannons somehow, but they have no idea that the president is here," Gunn said, and went on.

"They just want to shatter this base because we're blocking their access to the heartland. Do you have any idea how much this war is costing them? It's no wonder their emperor has been sleeping for so many years! I'd want to sleep too if this is the best my army could do," Dobbs said, laughing heartily at his own joke.

The President glanced at Marcus, standing quietly beside the wall, but was unable to keep the boy's thousand-yard stare.

"I think we should consider pulling some reinforcements from the Silver Isle, the demons have largely given up on that one," the President said.

"We could, but that might give up the game right then and there," Gunn said. "Try to reinforce Sunstrike over our gold reserve? That would basically scream "the leadership is hiding here!""

"Sir, with all due respect, and I do mean that," Dobbs said, smirking, "I've served under four presidents now, and you all suffer from the same delusion: that because you were elected by the mob for your five years, that somehow you know how all people think. I need to tell you, Mr. President, the demons don't think like us. They're barbarians. They don't think strategically, and they don't listen to any kind of reason or diplomacy. You're worrying over nothing, and even considering defeat or surrender is unbecoming of a head of state. Leave the fighting to the fighting men, sir, and try to relax, we need you to give an address to the people soon," Dobbs said.

Marcus could watch no more. He made his way to the door, leaving the three most powerful people in Merryland to cower and console one another. One of his immense black wings itched, and he scratched it, yawning as he went past the two guards at their posts by the door.

"Marcus, wait up lad," General Gunn's fatherly voice called behind him. Marcus stopped to let the general catch up to him. General Gunn was tall and barrel-chested, with a grisly scar that ran across his face, just missing his left eye but running across his nose. Reconstructive surgery had helped, his nose being intact, but the red scar only drew attention to where the work had been done. "Is there anything at all you need, lad?" the man asked the boy. General Gunn was an old soldier and paid close attention to the material costs and logistics of war. Every soldier was valuable to him, but Marcus suspected he overestimated his troops' strength in the face of the demonic invasion. Still, he wasn't as much of a nationalistic fool as Dobbs.

"I'm alright, sir," Markus said, looking down tiredly at his boots.

"I know being cooped up in this building wears on you, but all the same, you need to hope we don't need your training and strength," the old man said.

"Permission to speak freely?" Marcus asked.

"You have no rank, boy, speak away, and come, let's walk," the general said, nodding his head as he began to step smartly.

"We hide behind these walls while the demons on the ground make their progress, distracting us with their metal snakes and air machines, like we're waiting for them to come and slaughter us. Why do we make this pantomime, putting our lives on the line for the president? Why am I not stationed with my brothers and sisters, protecting something more valuable? There's a chain of command, and the president is completely useless. We could continue to fight even without him," Marcus said.

"While I agree with you more than you realize, boy, the demons aren't as stupid as Dobbs thinks. They want the president badly. If they can capture him, they can force him to cede power to their empire, and then, in the eyes of the law, we would have to cease all military functions," the general said as they went down into the bowels of the building, where the barracks were stationed. Soldiers playing pool or wrestling threw sidelong glances at the winged fledgling and the general but kept their distance.

"That makes no sense," Marcus said as they went into his room. It was spartan, nothing but a bed and a few neat piles of clothing and books on the bare concrete floor. "The President can sign whatever treaty he wants, but the military will never give up the fight, not when so many Meridial people have died."

"It's not that simple, kid. The people put their trust in that weak, ineffectual little man. They think he's wise and virtuous, and he is the head of our civil republic. Our society works under the illusion that the people self-govern themselves by supposedly picking their leaders. If we go against what the democratically elected rulers of Merryland order, we threaten the moral fiber of this nation. I'm not so sure that most of our enlisted men would happily take up arms against their brothers when the Commander in Chief of their nation's armed forces declares the war is over, and I doubt the other generals and admirals would be too keen to pursue a civil war," General Gunn said.

"We're at war!" Marcus cried. "What does any of that enlightened nonsense matter? We have bloodthirsty monsters at the door, trying to do what they did to Zelendior a hundredfold. They mean to turn our country into an extension of their own accursed continent!"

"All that might be true, boy, but you need to see things from my perspective. If I were to convince Dobbs to go in on officially removing the president from command and nullifying the chain of authority, where would that leave us when we threw the demon scum back to their nation? Our democracy would be lost. The illusion would be broken instantly. If our chain of command can be subverted so easily in the face of danger, how strong is our republic, and why have so many died to defend it?" Gunn asked.

"That's the stupidest thing I've ever heard. You would relinquish power when the war was over," Marcus said.

"Would I? Are you sure? How about that fool, Dobbs? Do you trust him to have more power than he already has?" Gunn asked. Marcus tried to answer, but the old general put up a hand. "Standby, kid. These are the questions every fighting man asks himself, when he isn't worrying about where the bullets are coming from or where he's going to sleep. You might find yourself with a hell of a rank after this is all said and done. Leave the thinking to those of us who are burdened to do so, and let's hope things don't get as far as you're worrying," he said, and tapped the side of his head. He left Marcus's room, probably going to another meeting, and the fledgling boy sat down on his bed.

THE CANNONS OF MERRYLAND

On the wall was a large mace, hanging from a hook by its black thong. It had been forged by his ancestor, the founder of his country of Merryland, the Arch-Angel Meridial. Killed in the Rapture Wars over fifteen-hundred years ago in the continent formerly known as Sunmaria, now known as Demon Land, he had left behind a holy warrior, a paladin, to rule over his beloved Merryland, as well as several children, angel-human hybrids known as fledglings. The ancient fledglings were massive and filled with power like their angelic forefather, but so many generations later, Marcus and the three other remaining fledglings were no larger than the average human, though they still possessed a measure of their ancestor's strength.

It didn't matter though. Here in Fort Sunstrike, as on the Silver Isle and the Dragon's Keep, the fledglings were just another tool for the generals to move around on their Astitution Tables. To send to their deaths. This land had been ruled by angels once, and Marcus and the others were just the dregs left behind by the demons.

As Marcus brooded in his room, a small company of demonic Ghoul Troopers sat in their trench, waiting for the chance to advance. The word depression doesn't have much meaning to soldiers biding their time in between killing and running. Demons came in different genetic lineages, depending on who their ancestors possessed, or incarnated within. Vermin, the medic and radio expert, lay on his back, watching explosive cannonballs fly over their trench as if he wasn't trapped in a warzone, waiting for the order to advance. He was a fiend, descended from a demon that had taken over a human body, as most demons in the empire were. His horns faced forward, long and light red in the setting sunlight. His scaly skin was light green, and his sharp teeth were covered in the remnants of the tasteless rations he was slowly consuming.

Trex, a reptilian demon, descended from a creature resembling a large crocodile, hunched by the edge of the incline into the trench, quietly surveying the battlefield. He was studying a length of barbed wire that was stretched across a fallen sky urchin and a white, sunbaked boulder. However, it did not reach the boulder, for Trex had shot the soldiers erecting it dead. He was the sharpshooter for the regiment, but his rifle lay beside his scaly claws. The dark, pupilless eyes most demons had peered from either side of his scaly head, scanning for potential targets in their vicinity. Most of the enemy troops were huddled in Fort Sunstrike, but whenever another demonic warship went down, a clean-up crew inevitably followed. There were also snipers hidden amongst the hills.

Sarrow the Chin stood near his commander, Lieutenant Shatter Howler, cleaning his Soul-Scorcher. Sarrow was a simian demon, descended from a demon who had taken over a chimpanzee. His proportions were wirier and more angular than a regular chimp though, as demons, on possessing a body, hollowed them out and stretched them to suit their true forms. The fangs of the ape had been sharpened further and turned black by the process of incarnation, and his hands were reshaped into vicious claws, not too different from Vermin's.

And then there was the Lieutenant himself. Shatter was a chiropteran, a demon descended from a lineage of bat demons. His long ears were angled towards the fortress they were engaged in breaking, but his attitude was one of overwhelming lassitude. He couldn't help it. Not even two weeks ago, he had left his regiment behind in order to go home for a funeral for his older brother, Void. The military campaign hadn't been quite this advanced then; his regiment, the Corrupters, had been stationed in the Meridial city of Eggshank, which had fallen with remarkably little collateral damage initially. It was a nice occupation, living within a condemned civilization, even if he knew he would likely be the one putting the inhabitants of Eggshank to the sword once the rest of the country fell. It was definitely nicer than being told that you and your entire regiment were being moved to the siege of Fort Sunstrike.

"What are we waiting for, Shatter?" Sarrow asked, inspecting his Soul-Scorcher as he folded his oilcloth up.

"Orders," the chiropteran replied. He glanced at the large radio that Vermin was laying against, willing it to transmit orders, insults, any kind of acknowledgement of their existence whatsoever. They hadn't dismantled a single cannon since they had stolen into the warzone. They simply skulked across the battlefield, moving from piles of wreckage and corpses and trenches to still more wreckage and corpses every night, hoping against hope none of the ferocious Meridial cannons decided to drop a payload on their hiding place. They heard other squads die in metal and fire, they heard screaming and flesh being ripped apart. It seemed that every day brought another attempt by the higher-ups to send a sky urchin humming towards the fortress, trying to run the blockade of cannons. Each cannon was a miniature fortress, and while Shatter believed his boys could handle one, he had learned not to question his orders.

"Have we taken a single cannon?" Sarrow asked.

"Are you asking if we personally have?" Shatter replied.

"Of course not, sir," Sarrow said, his chin jutting out insolently. "It would just seem that perhaps the urchins would have better odds of reaching the fortress if they waited for a few cannons to be dismantled," he said.

"Or commandeered," Trex said, not budging from his vantage point. "Imagine the boom-boom on those big guns!"

"Look alive, we've got incoming," Shatter said, as a cannon a few miles off fired into the air.

"You would think they would go easier on their ammo," said Vermin, yawning as he pulled his HellsBreath blasters out of his twin holsters. Demonic weapons like the large Soul-Scorchers and the smaller, handgun-sized HellsBreath blasters were built to channel a demon's spirit into a searing, concussive blast of fire.

"I see them, northwest, coming to see what happened to their scavengers," Trex said, pulling his bulk back into the trench. He had his rifle in his claws, and quickly loaded a round. Shatter unshouldered his Soul-Scorcher as the sound of the truck became audible to the rest of his regiment. There were four surly soldiers riding in the roofless vehicle, all of them wearing dusty helmets and grey fatigues.

"Hold on, Trex," Shatter said as he watched the vehicle come to a stop. The human soldiers were all on edge, having driven across the warzone, and waited as a private in the backseat stood up, studying the surroundings with a pair of binoculars. Shatter lowered himself in the trench, motioning for his soldiers to do the same, but Trex wasn't watching him, his eye was affixed to his scope. Shatter cursed under his breath. He had been hoping to take the truck off the humans without a fuss.

"Take your shot!" he yelled as he heard the human scout point out the reptilian demon skulking in the trench to his commander.

"Boom-boom," Trex muttered as he pulled his trigger, barrel of his gun as steady as a flagpole.

Trex's rifle cracked the relative peace of the trench, making Shatter wince as the shell popped out. He didn't hear the boy in the armored vehicle scream, but he didn't need to.

"Corrupters, take them before they get up!" he barked as he seized his Soul-Scorcher and jumped up. His blast melted the windshield of the vehicle, burning the driver's face off as he screamed in shock and pain, his teeth blackening and his eyes melting into white pools that turned black as they caught fire while the soldier died. Vermin ran up the incline to the left, shrieking aggressively as he fired wildly at the enemy. The advantage of surprise was lost though as the remaining two humans escaped from their deathtrap, their adrenaline already on edge from their stressful drive from their outpost.

"Vermin you stupid whelp! Get back down here! I want that damned truck!" Shatter ordered as the fiend laughed gleefully, firing on the vehicle as the humans cowered behind it. Sarrow the Chin had his Soul-Scorcher aimed just above the vehicle, waiting for one of the humans to emerge, while Shatter kept his aimed at the boulder. They would break out from either position.

"Sir, they're going to call in back-up!" Vermin shouted, standing out in the open.

"They already have, you tiny moron," Trex grumbled, his scope trained on the other side of the vehicle. Something landed a few feet from Vermin as he shook his head in frustration.

"Grenade!" Sarrow shouted, and Vermin scrambled, nearly dropping his blasters as he jumped into the trench.

Shatter shook his head in disgust as the one of the humans took a wild shot from behind the vehicle as the grenade went off, exploding in a blast of fire and shrapnel. Shatter grinded his teeth together as his sensitive ears rang painfully, and Trex snarled in fury as his shot went wild, narrowly missing his target. "Vermin, what in Great Satan's name are you doing! Get up and start shooting!" Shatter growled, firing past the boulder as Sarrow fired a blast over the vehicle.

"Sir, I rolled my fucken' ankle," the fiend moaned.

"Lieutenant, permission to bomb the truck?" Trex asked.

"Negative, we fucking need it," Shatter said. He glanced at the sky. There was still an hour of daylight remaining, and their position was compromised. "Corrupters, prepare for melee," he said, and set his Soul-Scorcher down. His right arm was cybernetic, composed of agonized steel, which was metal hardened through the fusion of tormented souls, and he straightened it out. The panels and gears within it swiftly shifted and smoothed as it reshaped itself into its double-edged sword-mode. Trex growled and shouldered his rifle. He needed no weapon besides his own physical bulk, his long maw full of serrated teeth like steak knives, his thick, spiked tail, and his heavy claws. Sarrow pulled out a HellsBreath blaster of his own as well as massive knife. One of the humans stood up, firing in the direction of the trench, while the other ran for the side of the vehicle.

"Move!" Shatter cried, his wide, black batwings flapping out as he flew out of the trench. From his elevated position, he saw the machine guns the soldier was making a desperate play for, propped up against the seats. Shatter landed on the hood of the truck as the soldier seized one of the guns.

"What are you waiting for?" the soldier, barely a man, hollered at the other soldier. The other man, much older than his companion, with a beard and garish tattoos on his arms, glanced at the chiropteran demon standing over him, his sword-arm extended menacingly, his black, empty eyes glistening in the fading sunlight, his sash decorated with glittering medals, and his wings wide, like a shadow encroaching on his life. The old soldier threw his gun to the ground, his hands held high. Trex seized the other man off his feet and tore his head off in his mouth, the man's cry of fear choked off instantly.

"Good move, Beast," said Shatter, not lowering his sword as Sarrow stepped behind the remaining soldier, who was already spattered with the gore of the scout Trex had shot. Sarrow put his knife around the man's throat, whose lips pressed together as he tried not to show any fear.

"Your name, please," Shatter said, leaping from the hood, his blade still level as he walked towards the soldier.

"It's Charles," the human said. Shatter shifted his gaze from the human's blue eyes and lowered his sword-arm. It shifted smoothly back into its arm mode, and Shatter gestured towards the trench.

"Trex, go get Vermin, and park his sorry ass in the back of my truck," he said. Trex nodded and turned back to the trench, still snacking on the soldier he had killed.

"Sarrow, handcuff our husk friend, Charles, and get him in the backseat," Shatter commanded, and the simian nodded.

The two soldiers who had come to scavenge and execute any survivors of the fallen sky urchin still lay where Trex had shot them down the day before, and Shatter knelt over them, undoing their gun and ammo belts.

"Sir, apologies," Vermin said. Shatter turned to him. The young fiend was standing on his sprained ankle, which he had bandaged and treated with a healing spell, yet was clearly not ready to hold his weight. Even without his ensorcered eyes, Shatter would have been able to tell that the demon was in a lot of pain. His radio was strapped to his back, and he held his blasters as if he were ready to take commands.

Shatter shook his head in disgust.

"Scavenge these corpses, and then get off that fucking ankle," he said, and went to the vehicle. He opened the driver side door and threw the soldier with the charred face off his seat. Shatter stepped over him, climbing over his blindly-staring eyes as he took his seat. Sarrow removed the other corpse from the passenger side and set about raiding its pockets.

"Five minutes, we need to get moving!" Shatter said, breathing deeply. They were out in the open, a bad place for a demonic regiment to be in.

"Sir, do you hear...," Vermin said as a cannonball whistled through the air, slamming into the trench they had been huddled in and exploding with a deafening roar. The blast knocked the fiend off his feet and blew Shatter and Sarrow's hair back. They covered their faces instinctively, but much of the debris went over their heads, most of the cannonball's energy spent within the trench.

The radio in the vehicle was crackling, but Shatter turned to the prisoner.

"How much back-up is coming?" he demanded.

"None. Command said they would have a cannon target your position so we could escape in case there was trouble," Charles replied, keeping his eyes low.

"This hasn't been your first adventure, I'm guessing," Shatter said as Trex climbed onto the back of the vehicle and Vermin leapt into the seat beside the human.

"I been captured before, and I'll be captured again," Charles replied evenly.

"So, you've been a prisoner before?" Shatter asked as he shifted into reverse and backed away from the barbed wire.

"What makes you ask?" Charles asked, keeping his eyes low.

"You're too smart to be anything except a survivor," Shatter said, driving around the fallen sky urchin. Sky urchins were the main flying machines the Apollyonic Empire used to police their own cities, as well as to drop soldiers into active warzones. They came equipped with missiles, tractor beams, and entire suites of surveillance equipment.

"I've been a prisoner alright, but not of war. I was convicted of a crime, and joining up was an easy way to knock time off my sentence. You quickly learn how to talk to your captors when you're in prison, who to show respect to, and when to show your teeth," Charles replied, careful to keep his eyes down.

"You know, in demonic prisons, showing your teeth isn't just an expression," Vermin said, and smiled a sharp grin at the human prisoner, who couldn't help himself and met the demon's gaze.

"Vermin, don't talk to the prisoner!" Sarrow snapped.

"That's good, Charles. That means you know how this is going to go down then," Shatter said.

The prisoner was silent as they drove around the fallen sky urchin, studying the damage to it. It had taken a direct hit in its undercarriage, and the exploding cannonball had caused extensive damage, tearing a gaping spider web of destruction in the bottom. The metal was broken as if it were nothing more than paper.

"How far away is your outpost, Charles?" Shatter asked as he turned the vehicle away from the wreck.

"It's three miles from here, just north of this position. There are around fifteen troops stationed there," Charles said.

"Sir, you're not actually thinking about assaulting a full outpost without back-up?" Sarrow asked.

"Quiet, Sergeant," Shatter admonished, keeping his eyes ahead. There was a cannon looming to the west, its barrel swiveling around and around menacingly as it searched for a target, and to the east was a collection of wrecked trucks and an ophidia andiron, a demonic automaton. It had been hit by two cannonballs, and lay with shards of splintered, twisted metal all around it.

"Charles, know this. If we get to the outpost and it differs in any way from your intel, I will allow Trex to consume you like he did your friend," Shatter said coldly. He gestured to Vermin without looking back.

"Inform Ops of our day and tell them we're heading for an enemy outpost."

Vermin, who had been wearing his radio headphones around his neck all this time, slid them over his ears and adjusted the knobs on the radio console that was sitting in his lap. Shatter turned up the dial on the truck's radio, frowning at the empty static that greeted him.

"Charles, what was the name of the driver? Did he have a call-sign or something like that?" the lieutenant asked.

"With all due respect, they'll know it isn't him, Dickens had kind of a unique way of talking," Charles said.

"And why, pray tell, should I care for the advice a husk prisoner gives me?" Shatter asked.

"Because, sir, the way I see it, if I lie to you, I'm unlikely to survive this adventure," Charles said, looking up for the first time.

"This is Fiend-oh-three-six calling Doom-seven-six-seven-oh, do you copy?" Vermin said into his mic.

The outpost came into view just over a hill. A series of tents erected in the shadow of a cannon; Shatter fought the urge to take to the skies as Sarrow left the truck to scout ahead with his binoculars. The last thing Shatter wanted for his military career was a sniper's bullet cutting it short.

"This is Fiend-oh-three-six, we've killed seven husks, position compromised, one husk in chains. In sight of enemy base, over," Vermin said into his mic.

"They've got three more trucks, and I spotted two snipers on the hill, they're scouting the other direction though," Sarrow said as he bounded back on all fours. "I counted ten soldiers, maybe a few went into the cannon's structure," Sarrow went on, but Shatter climbed out of the truck.

"Trex, see if you can get a good shot on those snipers, and hold on it," Shatter ordered as he turned his attention on Vermin.

"Ops hasn't replied, sir," Vermin said, holding one of the earphones to his ear.

"Transmit again," Shatter said, and put his hand out to Sarrow, who handed his binoculars over.

"Sir, if you take out those snipers, you'll give away our position," the simian said as Shatter studied the enemy's camp ahead of them.

"You wanna die before we get within firing distance of the enemy?" Shatter asked, handing the binoculars back.

"I don't think we should move in to attack, not without any back-up," Sarrow said.

"Anything, Vermin?" Shatter said, ignoring Sarrow's concern.

"Negative, sir."

Shatter glanced at Trex. The huge reptilian demon lay on his stomach, unmoving, his rifle held steady, the scope against one of his demonic, empty eyes. If need be, he could sit there for days, weeks even, just calmly waiting for the chance to move. His metabolism was so slow that the meal he had made of the human soldier would sustain him for months, even as he bore the load of their supplies on his back. He was the ultimate soldier, and he knew it.

"Sarrow, Ops is overwhelmed by the utter failure of this operation. They aren't going to get back to us. They're too busy trying to figure out how to get around the cannons," Shatter said. "Trex, hold onto your target. We're going to wait for nightfall."

"But sir, there's a reason no one has destroyed any of the cannons yet," Sarrow said.

"We've got something none of the other teams have taken yet," Shatter said, and gestured to Charles, sitting handcuffed beside Vermin. "In fact, Charles, if you want to tell us everything you know about the cannons, I might decide to set you free after we've killed all your friends."

"What do you want to know?" the human asked. He was no longer keeping his eyes down when he spoke to Shatter.

"How do we get into the substructure beneath the cannon?" Shatter asked.

"You would have to blast into the hill. They keep them supplied with personnel and ammunition through an underground rail system. The hills are fortified from within, allowing the soldiers to work the cannon no matter what's going on above ground," Charles explained.

Shatter kneeled down so he was eye-level with the human.

"Why did the Meridian's choose to fortify Fort Sunstrike with these cannons and not the more important bases, like the Dragon's Keep or Silver Isle?" he asked softly.

Charles smiled.

"You promised me you would set me free, but I have a hard time believing you. If I thought I could trust you, I would sell out this country in a heartbeat," he said.

Shatter stood up and savagely kicked the man with his heavy, pointed boot, throwing him onto his back with a surprised cry. The demon sneered at the human's hurt expression, the red mark of his boot running up his chin, into his cheek.

"Vermin, execute the prisoner. We're going to pull back and wait for night to settle. Trex, continue to hold the target, there's a good beast," Shatter said, patting the reptilian on the shoulder as he returned to the truck.

Shatter thought of his younger brother, Splinter, as he heard Charles's sad whine of horror and pain as Vermin discharged his HellsBreath blasters into the human's mouth. Splinter had decided to ditch their brother, Void's funeral, choosing to go to a ceremony at some human church with his stupid human girlfriend instead. Shatter had never had any love for the humans of the empire, but it wasn't until he enlisted with the Ghoul Troopers that he learned to despise them. Maybe someday his stupid little brother would understand.

Merryland was a country that was founded before the Rapture Wars, nearly two-thousand years ago. When the demonic souls were released from their otherworldly prison by the renegade angel, Apollyon, there were very few incarnations in Merryland. What demons that were there, Shatter and every other citizen of the Apollyonic Empire were taught, were slaughtered in a panicked genocide. They had been at war ever since, the demons and the rest of the world, and while the demonic empire had swallowed the entire continent of Sunmaria, warping it into Demon Land, it had made little progress in gaining footholds in the other continents of Erde.

Shatter and other demons didn't hate humans for their atrocities towards their kind; it was only natural for the humans to fear that which had stolen the bodies of their lovers, their children, their livestock, to hate that which their angelic overlords hated, that which had taken those same overlords from them. No, Shatter didn't hate the humans because they were humans. All demons lived to perpetuate the ideal they called the Struggle. Their souls were all that remained of the Great Satan, whose soul was shattered when he was banished from Heaven. They hated the humans because it was their duty to do so. They had invaded the physical world, and if they didn't continue the conquest of Erde, the sacrifices of Great Satan's fall and Apollyon's mercy would be in vain, for the true inhabitants of Erde would never allow the aberrations that the demons were to exist alongside them. Shatter saw the fear and revulsion in the eyes of his combatants when he got close to them, the contempt they showed even as he flew after them, shrieking in fury, drenched in the blood of their fellows.

The hatred was mutual, and Shatter ignored the pang of guilt he felt as he watched Vermin throw Charles's body into the back of the truck with the rest of the dead humans. He had gotten exactly what he deserved, the filthy, weak husk. Besides, Shatter had never planned to release him. He desperately needed every dead human he could get his claws on.

His ears twitched.

"Vermin, someone is on the radio," Shatter said.

The tech limped to his radio, knowing better than to question Shatter's hearing.

"This is Fiend oh-three-six, repeat please, over," Vermin said into his mouthpiece as he clapped his headphones over his ears. The radio crackled in response. "Sir, they want to address you directly," the fiend said, and handed Shatter the headpiece.

"This is Ghoulking eight-nine-nine, over," Shatter said, his heart beating heavily.

The voice from the radio, though drowned by static, was immediately familiar. It was General Storm, and Shatter felt relief flood his body as he spoke.

"This is Scar oh-three, we're dealing with a situation back home, pulling zzzt hardware across the sea, hold your position, being remanded to Admiral zzzt," the General said, his final words lost in the static.

"I'm losing you!" Shatter yelled into the mouthpiece and gritted his teeth in frustration. He pulled the headset off and held it uselessly, feeling lost in the vast battlefield. He listened to cannons in the distance firing their payloads, bursts of gunfire, shouted orders, and the silence in between. The cannon they had their attention set on was still, the outpost they were poised to attack as much in the dark as to their situation as they were, and the entire scenario completely out of control.

"Anything of use?" Sarrow the Chin asked.

Shatter shook his head.

"Shit, man," The Chin said. He pulled a box of cigarettes out of his helmet's strap.

Shatter's revery passed, and he was back in control. He could feel Trex's eye, the one that wasn't fixed on his sniper scope, focused on him. Vermin was back on the ground by the truck, treating his sprained ankle again. Shatter was responsible for these men, a duty that no one else in command seemed to care about. *Hold your position.* They had enough rations for another few weeks, but morale was only as high as his own confidence. It was no secret that the orders had been scarce and the feedback to their reports were non-existent since they were dropped to the edge of this warzone. Shatter's resolve was the only thing keeping his men focused, and he knew that like most things in the empire, the only way to succeed against everything that wanted so desperately for you to fail was to grit your teeth and seize it yourself, even if you died in the attempt. That was the true meaning of the Struggle.

"Vermin, make yourself useful and give me a skeleton crew, Trex wait for my order. After Trex takes out those snipers, get in the truck," he ordered, and Sarrow went to assist the fiend as he limped to the truck.

Vermin and Sarrow dragged the dead bodies to where Charles's dead body lay, his bloodshot eyes watching the dusty sky pass on above him. Vermin was not a necromancer, or really much of a sorcerer at all. Like most demons, he had a natural affinity for magic not relating to the five elements of air, fire, water, earth, and aether. Being otherworldly in origin, they could manipulate darkness, souls, and harness different, lower forms of magic, such as illusion casting and divination, all by channeling their demonic essence into different forms. Vermin, being trained as a medic, was able to treat wounds with his essence, and was also able to perform a weak rite that could turn any dead body into a puppet under his control. A weak form of necromancy, the corpses would be given a small sliver of the caster's essence, which would animate them to be able to move under his command for a limited time. Skeleton crews could also be sent without any direct control, but this was dangerous at best, as the reanimated fighters could not distinguish between their targets or their allies. They were only used in moments of duress.

"Snipers are moving," Trex called to Shatter. His rifle moved slightly as he followed his targets.

"They've gone into the cannon's superstructure. Now there are two other snipers taking their places."

"They must trade off every few hours," Shatter said. "Now we know there's a door, at least. How's my skeleton crew coming?"

Vermin was crouched above one of the dead bodies, a knife in one hand, his other wrist dripping blood onto the corpse. He smeared his blood onto each of their faces, wishing there was time to flay the flesh from their skulls. It was much easier to control a skeleton crew when the link was made directly with their dry bones. He licked the blood from his gushing wrist, spreading it across his face, and whispered a healing spell. Green light enveloped his wrist, and the cut began to close, the throbbing vein to clot.

"Give the word, and they'll rise up," Vermin said.

"Send 'em down, and when they're close enough to the camp, cut 'em loose," Shatter said as he and Sarrow climbed into the truck.

"I can take both of the snipers out without a problem. They aren't even looking for targets, the one is smoking, the other is sleeping," Trex called out.

"They think they're in a secure place, even though two teams went missing," Sarrow said, blowing smoke out of his black lips.

"Sir, are we arming these stiffs?" Vermin asked.

"No, we're keeping their gear. Send them over now, we need whatever break we can get," Shatter said.

"So marked, arise by my word, stir from your sleep, death is my only order for thee," Vermin spoke to the corpses, his hands contorted into mystical shapes. Red light engulfed his hands, and the dead bodies on the ground twitched, being jolted to a simulacrum of life. The spell was a weak one and was only constructed to animate bones. The muscles, organs, and flesh were not stimulated by the dark magic, and so weighed down on the lightweight spell, but Vermin was able to get them off the ground. The six dead men stared blankly at him, their heads flopping back and to the sides, drool spilling from their hanging mouths. Vermin gestured towards the human camp in the valley with one of his hands, and spun the other aggressively, driving the spell onwards. The skeleton crew slouched away, shambling in a loose single file that failed to hold together as they stumbled down the hillside. Shatter watched them go, staggering towards their late camp as Vermin held his glowing hands out, his hands shaking as the skeleton crew got further and further away from him.

"Good job, Verm. Cut the bastards loose and get in here. Trex, take out the snipers and get in the back of the truck!" Shatter ordered as he turned the key in the ignition. Vermin crossed his arms, and the red lights went out from around his claws. He jumped into the backseat of the truck as the report of Trex's rifle echoed through the newborn night. His second shot drowned out a distant cannon's roar, and the huge reptilian demon laughed grimly as he jumped into the bed of the truck. He settled himself over Vermin's seat as he held his rifle out, ready to take another shot as the truck drove down the hill.

The tents came to life as the two rifle shots took out the snipers. Lanterns came on, and soldiers emerged, guns in hand. They were met by six of their missing comrades, all of them shambling forward, two of them with bloated, purple heads, mouths filled with flies and maggots, and gaping gunshot wounds in their foreheads, whatever was left of their brains dripping out of their shattered skulls. The other four were similarly grisly, their faces scorched black by Soul-Scorcher fire, and Charles with his mouth nothing more than a hole burned straight through his head. Bullets had no effect on them, and even when one of them had his kneecap shot, he continued to crawl, dragging his body through the dirt with his hands. One man screamed as three of the skeleton crew caught him, holding him in place as they sank their teeth into his face and throat, his blood staining them as they tore into him. The headlights of the stolen truck flooded the camp, and even as the soldiers of the outpost coalesced into a defensible position, shooting the legs and arms of the reanimated soldiers, Vermin's HellsBreath blasters lit up the night along with Sarrow's Soul-Scorcher, blasting the soldiers where they stood. Trex bellowed into the night and leapt from the bed of the truck, having grabbed the two machine guns from the back of the truck. He opened fire, still roaring as the heavy human weapons sounded in his tremendous arms, making his massive girth shake as the human soldiers danced before him, their bodies torn to shreds by the bullets. Some of them managed to turn their weapons towards the reptilian demon as he gunned them down, but their shots counted for nothing as the demonic sneak attack destroyed them. Shatter emerged from the truck, kicking aside the twitching wet remains of the skeleton crew and studying the tents of the outpost. His arm reformed itself into its sword-mode, and he slashed at the canvas of the tents, confirming that there were no more soldiers in hiding here. He heard a click from the hill and glanced in time to see a telescope escaping back into the cannon's superstructure.

"Trex, lead us to the door you saw," Shatter ordered.

"Not much left to make another skeleton crew out of, eh boss?" Vermin said, kicking a dead human's head.

In Fort Sunstrike, General Gunn received the news of the attack on the cannon in his office quietly. He dismissed the radio tech and flicked his Astitution Table on, the red light coloring his pale face in the relative darkness of his office. The cannons were attacked occasionally. They were designed to be attacked, designed and placed so they would be attacked, would have to be attacked, all while Fort Sunstrike grimly stood its ground in the middle of the raging cannons. So far, for the three months the fortress had been under siege, the cannons had done better than even General Gunn had expected them to do. They had held the demons off completely, made a joke of their shock and awe tactics. When the invasion had first begun two years ago, he had pushed for cannons to be installed all across the country, but the cost had been prohibitive, and the Parliament had refused to allocate the necessary funds.

As much as President Novak wanted to believe nationalist fools like General Dobbs, Gunn knew that the bottom line could not be denied: the war was going badly.

The truth of the matter was that it didn't matter if they broke Fort Sunstrike and captured the president. If the demons pulled their heads out of their bleeding asses, they would realize that decimating Merryland's proud cities and infrastructure would effectively cause them to be unable to recover from the damage of the invasion. Already, enough destruction had been wrought by the enemy's sorcerers and Ghoul Troopers that the national debt would take a century to recover from, and as far as Gunn was concerned, the enemy was just getting started. Monitoring the propaganda and media of Demon Land, their society was one that thrived on jingoism and a robust victim complex. They justified everything they did against their holy "Struggle". Invading other countries was necessary because they were hated and despised by their neighbors. Subjugating the humans living in their cities was necessary because demons could expect nothing but hatred and cruelty from the others who shared Erde with them. Never mind that the world might have accepted demonkind after two-thousand years if they had shown any level of empathy or civilization after their massacre of the angels.

In the end, as Gunn saw it, Merryland's best chance was just to hold on to every single armament and position they had and pray to the soul of Meridial for strength. Considering their god and founder was a dead angel, perhaps they were doomed.

But the cannons, unlike their thunder tanks and jets, had held out up until now. The demonic sky urchins couldn't get close enough without being detected to unleash their payloads, and they never got too far when they tried to maneuver out of the way of the missiles that were fired by the cannons. Dodging one simply wasn't good enough when you were being fired on by as many as four cannons at a time. It was true that the hilly terrain of Fort Sunstrike was part of what made its cannon defenses so effective, but there was no reason why the rest of the country couldn't be defended in the same way.

Except that the demons had just engaged one of his precious cannons. The incursion couldn't be successful, that much was certain, and the fact that the demonic units were so busy battling the individual cannons that they would never reach the fortress was part of the point, but still, the cannons were so secure that he had begun to think the enemy might completely break themselves against them. The cannon that was under attack was marked in red. A single red cannon in a sea of blue. The battlefield was mapped in a grid, with Fort Sunstrike at its center. The lines were set three miles apart, with each zone another three miles, making it possible for the cannons to be clearly located on the map. With nine parallel lines, the warzone of Fort Sunstrike covered a perimeter of thirty-six miles, with the fortress standing on the sixth parallel, at position 5-18. The cannon that was under attack was at position 7-25. Assuming this demonic squad had been released near the perimeter, they had straggled across the battlefield with no success, surviving the Meridial defenses for weeks, before finally attacking a cannon. Had they not engaged their enemy up until now? It didn't really matter, Gunn thought as he considered his options. Assuming the demons captured the cannon, they were hopelessly outgunned. If Gunn gave the word, four other cannons would fire their payloads at it, leaving nothing but a burned hill with a hunk of black, melted metal burnt over it. The demons could hit the fortress if they captured the cannon, but considering they weren't trained in how to load and fire it, let alone how to package and arm the cannonballs, Gunn wasn't too worried about that. And that was assuming there even were enough armaments left for the demons to use. Gunn pushed a few buttons on the edge of the table, and the rail route to the cannon turned green, the details of its manifest displayed above it. They had gotten a delivery that morning, and judging from the single strike that cannon had made that day, had plenty to spare. He could always reinforce the cannon station, move troops from one of the other cannons along the railway system, forcing the demons to retreat or risk defeat or, even more tantalizing for Gunn, capture. As much as he wanted to give that order, he felt as though depriving any of the cannons of their manpower was a deadly mistake. The cannons were the only thing keeping the heart of Merryland safe, and he didn't dare to jeopardize them. His only other option was to wait. If the cannon fell, he would give the order to destroy it, as well as to collapse the tunnel. Destroying the cannon, giving up an essential part of their defense net, was useless if the underground rail system was left exposed, leading straight to the fortress. The general returned to his desk, eyeing a cigar as he switched on his own radio and made contact with the besieged cannon.

Trex had torn the door off its hinges after he dented it, pounding aimlessly against the hillside as they searched for the portal. It hadn't been a matter of where it was so much as how to open it, and even though Shatter regretted the destruction of the door, he didn't seriously expect to be able to hold the cannon for any length of time.

"Stay back!" a human hollered hoarsely up at them, and Shatter kneeled near the portal, listening to his foes in the cannon station with his superior hearing. Another soldier was talking frantically into a microphone, while the clicking of bullets being loaded into a magazine sounded from another corner. Shatter activated his Soul-Scorcher, feeling its pull on his demonic essence.

"My name is Shatter Howler, Lieutenant in the Apollyonic Army. Surrender this cannon to me, and I promise you will be dealt with mercifully," he shouted down, trying to see where the scaffolding led. The only answer was a gunshot that sent a bullet whistling past his ear.

"What's the call, boss?" Sarrow asked, glancing from Trex to Vermin.

"The distance from their battle stations to our position is pretty far, we'll have to move hard and fast since we won't have any cover. We need to get in there, and we need to kill those fuckers before they get any reinforcements," Shatter said, and made as if to go into the portal.

"Sir, wait," Vermin said, taking out his blasters. "Are you sure we should be going in there? What if the humans make another cannon blow it up?"

"Kid, these cannons are too important to their defenses. They aren't going to risk one just because a couple of demons took one, they'll fight to the death to take it back, trust me," Shatter said, and ducked into the doorway. Sarrow clapped Vermin on the shoulder as he followed his commander.

"Afraid of fighting humans now?" he asked as Shatter's Soul-Scorcher hissed within the hill. The human soldiers inside the hill hollered orders and panicked, firing wildly as Sarrow and Trex joined Shatter in bombarding them through the metal bars of the scaffolding. A bullet struck Shatter's chest, throwing him back even as his body armor absorbed the shot. Vermin stopped shooting to make sure Shatter got back up and screeched as one of his shots struck a crate that ignited as the Hellfire tore through it.

"Exploding powder!" Trex shouted and began barrelling down the make-shift steps that led down into the hill.

General Dobbs burst into General Gunn's office, startling the older man.

"I've been informed you're monitoring the situation with the cannon on your own," Dunn said irritably, standing in the doorway.

"That I am, Dobbs. Our boys are holding the station just fine. I've got several teams on standby, ready to intercept if things go sideways," Gunn said, and took a drag on his cigar.

"What do you mean, 'intercept'?" Dobbs demanded.

"Either we reinforce the position through the railway by pulling soldiers from other stations or we take it out. We are not letting those demons have one of our cannons," Gunn said.

"They have no chance, Gunn. There's four of them for Jane's sake! One of them is a stupid reptile. You are looking to jeopardize our defenses for nothing."

"Dobbs, I've never asked you before. Are you dense?" Gunn asked.

"Did I miss something?" Dobbs said and flicked on the lights. "We're both in command of this mission, Bruce."

"Do you have an issue with our boys holding onto our cannons?" Gunn asked.

General Dobbs was at a loss, staring incredulously at the other man.

"Gunn, every man has his job at the cannon. We can't be moving them around willy-nilly, and you can't seriously be considering an attack on our own cannon. It isn't like we can just go and repair them after we've gotten rid of those worthless demons."

"Dobbs, you seem to be under the misapprehension that the enemy is incompetent, weak, and stupid. Brutish and cruel, I think you called them at a meeting. You talk about our greatest foes like you're an exterminator dealing with roaches, but the more I have to tolerate you, the more I think we should just duel so I can end your stupidity," Gunn said, his heavy cigar smoke filling the room.

"Are you suggesting the demons are anything but a pestilence? You're insane to think that we could ever lose a single cannon to them. Besides, this is what the enemy wants. That little gaggle of monsters sees back-up arriving on the railway, and that's when they give the go-ahead for their flying saucers to come back!"

"Dobbs, they aren't a 'gaggle'. These bastards are trained, instinctive killers. They took out our entire outpost without a fight and are in the process of breaking through our armor. That cannon is a breaking point," Gunn said.

"They cheated to pull that off! Didn't you hear the transmission?" Dobbs argued. General Bruce Gunn ignored the mustachioed man.

"Teams D-12 and F-22, prepare to transfer to 7-25, breach in progress," he said into his mouthpiece.

"Belay that order!" Dobbs shouted and banged his fist on the desk. The books and penholders jumped, the contents of the older man's workspace thrown in disarray. He reached for Gunn's headpiece, but Gunn punched Dobbs in his jaw.

"You son of a whore," the other general fumed, and stormed out.

"Hang in there, 7-25, help is coming," Gunn said, and climbed to his feet. He lightly touched the gun in his holster as he snuffed his cigar in its wooden ash bowl and went in pursuit of Dobbs. He would be damned if there would be conflicting orders in the radio room. The men in that cannon station had enough trouble from the invading demons without command ruining their day further.

"Cease fire!" yelled the same man who had hollered at Shatter to stay back. The gunfire stopped almost instantly, and Shatter put up a hand. There was one man on the ground, badly burned from the chemical explosion, and another bent over him, trying to treat him. Another was crouched under the control panel for the cannon, a rifle held in his trembling hands. Another peeked from behind a box, his headset held in one hand, a pistol in another. Three other soldiers had their guns aimed at the four demons, but as far as Shatter could tell, these soldiers hadn't handled a rifle in years. They trembled as the four demon Ghoul Troopers sneered at them, the barrels of their weapons still smoking from their discharge.

Shatter pointed his Soul-Scorcher at one of the soldiers aiming his rifle at them. Colorful medals were affixed to his chest, and he wore a red hat with a dragon's head embroidered on it.

"Are you the scumbag that actually managed to hit me?" Shatter demanded.

"No, that would be the corporal under the terminal," the man said. "I am the sergeant in charge of this installation, and I have been ordered to surrender myself to you in exchange for my men's lives," he said, and gulped as the demons looked at one another in surprise.

Chapter 2: Breaking Point

Markus sat at his bench in the mess hall, morosely stirring his gruel as he slowly worked on a drawing on his little pad. Soldiers wandered in and out, and most of them sat, talking boisterously as they ate their food. No one sat alone like Markus, and he was careful not to catch anyone's eye. He didn't want company. The hours in the fortress passed like nails in his flesh, and it was all he could do to keep his mind occupied. Unlike the other guys stationed in the fortress, he was not on call, and had no rank in the army. At any moment, any of the shouting and dancing fools in the mess hall could be transferred to one of the cannon stations across the battlefield, shuttled out of the safe fortress to man one of the big guns at a whim.

And the transfers did happen, constantly men were shuttled to the fortress to be relieved by fresh boys, ready to assume their stations under the cannons. Markus had no strong desire to work one of the cannons, but he was tired of walking the hallways of the fortress, tired of the generals checking up on him as if they really cared about how he was feeling or truly wanted to know him. He was a weapon, and his mental health was secondary to his ability to singlehandedly turn the tide in a pitched battle with the demonic legions if it came down to that.

"Hey angel-boy, you drawing a pretty, pretty picture for your room?" a soldier said, and his two friends laughed as they passed.

Markus bit his lip, and pressed his pencil down hard enough that the tip broke. He missed his fellow fledglings. Maria with her wry wit and blazing red hair was too much for most men to handle, especially when she became enraged, which was often. She didn't take kindly to men talking to her just because they wanted to have sex with her, which, as far as she was concerned, was all men, with notable exceptions. Markus was one such exception, and she always knew how he was feeling, which was usually down.

"Just remember, Marky, we're gonna outlive most of these bastards," she was fond of saying.

When she was given the ring of Meridial, a relic the angel had been given to his first-born child, the fledgling named Mellenia, she hadn't been satisfied.

"Why do you give us the tokens of our birthright only now, when Merryland is under attack?" she had demanded of the steward, fitting the ring, forged for a much larger finger than any of hers, to the hilt of her sword. She wasn't insane or destructive and hadn't brought up her frustrations during the public ceremony where they had been given their relics with which they would defend the pressure points of Merryland against the demons' Apollyonic Empire. Still though, even though she took seriously the role she and the other three fledglings of the Arch-Angel Meridial played in the defense and national character of Merryland, she hated the president and the entire administration.

Things couldn't be more different with Bobbi-Anna, Maria's aunt. Older than her niece by thirty years, she was the oldest fledgling alive in the world, let alone Merryland, which really wasn't saying much, as there were only a few surviving angelic bloodlines that had survived the purges following the end of the Rapture Wars. Bobbi-Anna was forty-eight, and though that was middle-aged for a human, for a fledgling, that was maybe a quarter of her lifespan. The angelic genes sometimes skipped a few generations, but Maria and Bobbi-Anna's family had the honor of two fledglings in only two, which as practically unheard of. Markus didn't particularly care for Bobbi-Anna. She always had something to say about him, from his indifference to her patriotism, to his lack of passion for his training, to the way he wore his hair. She was jealous of the power he had been blessed with, and he knew that she had only been given the armor of Meridial's paladin because of her seniority. It didn't matter, though. Markus knew she seethed that he was given not only Asdeev, the great mace that Meridial had wielded himself against the demon scum, but also the defense of the president.

And then there was Tolbert. Tolbert was stationed with Maria at the Dragon's Keep merely because on his own, he was borderline suicidal. Originally from a small hamlet in Demon Land called Horntown, his family had kept the secret of their descent from one of Meridial's fledglings quiet for centuries, severing the wings of their fledgling babies at birth to shield them from the Scourge, the demonic police force. Tolbert had no wings, and no family either. When he was still a child, he incinerated a little girl in a fit of rage with a beam of energy he fired from his eyes, outing him instantly. In Demon Land, there is practically nowhere to hide from the Scourge or its auxiliary intelligence division, the Suppression Force, once they determine that you're a threat to the empire. And so it was that Tolbert was taken away by the Scourge as a child and subjected to tests that were indistinguishable from the torturous procedures the demonic scum meted out to their prisoners of war. His parents being executed in front of him was just the start of his suffering, and Markus felt that the double agent that had rescued Tolbert had done little to help the boy if all Merryland was going to do was slap a pair of artificial wings on his scabbed stubs the second they were invaded by their erstwhile enemies.

Maria and Markus saw Tolbert as their little brother even though none of them were directly related. They had taught him how to fly, demonstrating how to flap his wings, how to angle his body into the wind in order to turn and glide, as well as how to fight and defend while airborne. They were trained from the moment they were able to walk, and he had a lot to catch up on. More importantly though, for Markus anyway, was Tolbert's obsession with card games. "Monster Massacre", to be specific. It was a collectible trading card game played with cards pulled from packs of random cards, all of which depicted horrific monsters or spells the players could cast on each other's cards. Monster Massacre was what Markus and Maria bonded with Tolbert over, and Markus just wanted the war to end so that they could all just get back to playing their card games again.

Markus left the mess hall, trying his damndest to tune out the voice of the soldier who had had the gall to call him "angel-boy" as if it were an insult. He hated his station in Fort Sunstrike if only because it made the difference the state placed on his personhood all the more stark and real. Almost on cue, General Gunn burst from the stairwell, and Markus stopped to face him.

"Just the man I'm looking for," the older man said. "Don't stop, let's continue on to your room." Markus shrugged and continued walking. The general was always stopping him to chit-chat, and Markus wasn't about to start lecturing him on how he chose to spend his time. It wasn't as if Markus had anything better to do than to wait around for the Dobbs and Gunn Clown Show to figure its shit out and decide when his role in their beautiful defense plan would come.

"Markus, I need to know where you stand," General Gunn said as he closed Markus's door behind him.

"Stand on what?" Markus asked as he flopped onto his bed. The springs sang painfully as he stretched out, directing his attention at a pencil drawing of Fort Sunstrike on fire. He was no great artist, but had done a good enough job at distinguishing the walls of the fort and depicting its burning banners.

"A squad of demons has taken over one of our cannons," the general said breathlessly, with seemingly a trillion more words struggling to explode from him.

"So? Have you sent reinforcements already? What's it to do with me?" Markus asked.

"My orders were to move some soldiers from a nearby cannon, but Dobbs, in his infinite wisdom, believed the cannon would hold. When it fell and the demon lieutenant shrieked in our colonel's headset, I tried to give the order to destroy the cannon and bury the fuckers, but Dobbs gave a conflicting order right there in the fucking command center, and now our boys are doing nothing as the demons are starting to rally and gather. I need to know I can count on you, kid," Gunn pressed.

"What choice do I have?" Markus asked.

"Dobbs will probably tell you to stay here and guard the President until the very end, but I want you to get on that shuttle and crucify those bastards," Gunn said.

Markus pressed his head into his bed so he could see his mace, hanging from a hook on the wall.

"I mean, whatever dude. I'm sure those demons won't stand a chance against me. I don't know why you guys keep us locked away while the rest of the country burns. I probably could have put the hurt on them when they decided to bomb Eggshank, if even I couldn't have saved everyone," Markus said.

"You fledglings are important assets, and we can't afford to lose any of you. Someday, maybe soon, I think it would behoove me to discuss military policy with you, but for now, you need to buckle on your belt and get to the shuttle. Bring me the lieutenant's head," Gunn said.

"Is that an order?" Markus asked as he got up and grabbed the belt that hung beneath Asdeev.

"You bet your ass it is," Dobbs growled.

Vermin went around the cannon station, handing out the medals he had plucked from the dead human corporal's uniform. Shatter took one that was shaped like a spiked mace-head, and smiled grimly at Vermin as he went on to Trex, who had sustained a gunshot to the head. Vermin had already treated him, and the reptilian weakly accepted a medal as he lay beside his shattered helmet.

"You think he'll be okay?" Sarrow asked Shatter, turning over his own trophy in his paws, a simple medal that was shaped like a purple star.

"I don't know," Shatter said. He was sitting beside Vermin's radio, holding the headset close to one of his long bat-ears. "This is Ghoulking eight-nine-nine calling any squad on this frequency to my position, respond if you can hear me, over," he said into the mic, his heart beating as he silently prayed for a response. The relative silence beneath the cannon was suffocating for him after the gun fire and screaming that had occurred there not even two minutes ago.

Sarrow went towards the back of the station, where a tunnel yawned like the maw of a fossilized subterranean monster. He knelt down, studying the rails that would bring reinforcements into the cannon. Gazing into the tunnel, Sarrow could see that there were three branching paths that the rail took, and he wondered which one would take them closer to the fortress.

"I repeat, this is Ghoulking eight-nine-nine, I'm reading you, repeat your message, over," Shatter said into the mic.

Vermin contorted his fingers over Trex's head, generating a green glyph above his bullet wound. He had extracted the bullet already, and now he was gently willing the wound to heal. The shot had struck the great demon's skull, but hadn't gone any further. Still though, Trex was bleeding internally, and Vermin was still working to extract the bone fragments even as he worked to heal the wound as quickly as he could.

"We've got back-up coming," Shatter said to Sarrow as the simian came out of the tunnel. "What did you find?"

"We cannot go into the tunnel, not even if we hijack a shuttle from human reinforcements," Sarrow said. Shatter followed his loyal sergeant to the tunnel and looked where he indicated. There, attached to the tunnel ceiling by strong metal wire hung what was unmistakably TNT, and Shatter gave a low screech, using his echolocation to scan further into the tunnel. He gave a low squeak of dismay as his fears were confirmed.

"They've wired the entire tunnel system to blow just in case it was ever compromised," Sarrow said as Shatter's ears drooped.

"We're fucked," Shatter said. He went back into the station, kicking aside the severed head of the corporal who had tried to surrender to him. The controls of the cannon seemed simple enough, even covered in the blood of the soldier Trex had splattered against them. There were three periscopes around the station, and the cannon's head was controlled with two separate wheels. A simple LCD image of the cannon's barrel moved as Shatter lightly moved one of the wheels.

"One wheel rotates the barrel around, the other moves it up and down," he muttered. There were two more buttons, and Shatter puzzled over which was the button to fire a payload, and why there would be another button.

"All we can do now is wait for the big guy to wake up," Vermin said.

Shatter sighed deeply. There was a small pile of bombshells near the control panel, and he stepped over the soldier Sarrow had thrown against it after tearing his throat out. The dead soldier's bloodshot eyes seemed to watch Shatter vengefully as he ran his nails over the black face of one of the bombshells. As far as he could tell, they were all ready to launch, and were likely sent by shuttle that way. It would take two of them to move one, unless Trex decided to wake up.

"What do you want to do, Boss?" Sarrow asked.

"I don't know. General Storm couldn't even talk to me, the static was so bad. We can probably lob a shot at the fortress or another cannon, but what's the point if they're abandoning us out here?" he asked.

"Wait, what?" Vermin asked.

Almost as if on cue, the headset in Shatter's hand crackled.

"Back-up's here, arm yourself in case it's a trap," Shatter said. Vermin drew one of his blasters and climbed the scaffolding.

"Do you think we're safe down here?" Sarrow asked.

"Besides the open tunnel that will be bringing a death squad to exterminate us?" Shatter asked.

"I mean, we can build a barricade and hold out for a long time. I'm more concerned about them firing on this place, bringing the cannon down on us."

"No Sarrow, they won't blow up one of their precious cannons," Shatter said, watching as Vermin opened the portal.

"Shatter?" a familiar voice called, and Sarrow relaxed.

"What are the chances?" the simian said.

A fiend with red skin and green horns stepped onto the scaffolding, and Shatter breathed a sigh of relief.

"Blusterfew, please tell me you're not alone," he said.

"No can do, Lieutenant," the fiend said, descending with Vermin. The two fiends dropped down, and he nodded to Vermin.

"Who's this rookie?" he asked.

"Private Vermin, he's a good kid. He's my healer. That sleeping monster over there is Trex, hopefully he'll be back on his feet thanks to the kid's talents," Shatter said.

"When you told me you'd taken a cannon, I knew there would be casualties," Blusterfew said sadly.

"We were in boot camp together," Sarrow said to Vermin, who looked lost.

"Where's the rest of your squad?" Shatter asked.

"All gone. We were ambushed shortly after the General announced they were moving most of our hardware back to contain the situation in Duskrim," Blusterfew said.

"What was that all about?" Sarrow asked.

"No one has any idea. We ran into the Boneshredders out there, and we slaughtered our way to a different cannon, but their snipers took out too many of us, and then we had to pull back. The Boneshredders got moved to back up another squad, and then the call came."

"So what, did the Meridians hit us back home?" Vermin asked.

"No one knows, but probably not," Sarrow said glumly.

"So we're supposed to just...survive until they come back for us," Vermin said.

The stale air in the cannon station was heavier than the silence that followed. Shatter turned away as Vermin's eyes strayed to him. He could practically feel Sarrow's shoulders slump, and he could hear the low rumble of Trex's labored breathing as he lay on his back.

"Where are you from?" Bluserfew asked Vermin.

"I come from Shacklesburgh. My parents own a farm there, and I joined up to get them a business grant," Vermin said. "My dad never served, and my mother didn't want me to do it, but I knew how badly they needed the money. I just hope I make it back to them," he said.

"We've all got reasons why we're fighting," Blusterfew said.

"Our destiny is to be as Great Satan was, the Great Destroyer. I joined to help destroy our enemies in Merryland," Sarrow said proudly.

"You guys know all about me, but Vermin, you didn't meet me until you were assigned to me in Eggshank," Shatter said, still facing away from his men. "I joined up because my dad is Senator Malekarm, and he's got big plans for my brother and me. I'm here to earn a high enough rank to help him with his ambitions, but to be honest, I don't even give a fuck about all that power-hungry-destroyer of worlds shit they holler at us all our lives. I just want to gut our enemies and get everyone home now," Shatter said.

He turned around swallowing as hard as he could. It didn't matter what command was doing. He was still in charge of these men, damn it.

"We're taking a shot at that fortress, and if they want to shoot back, that's on them," Shatter said. "Vermin, get on those periscopes and tell me which direction the fortress is in," he commanded. "And Bluster, help me load this big fucking gun," he said to his friend.

Blusterfew's uniform was filthier than Shatter's, with dried guts and blood crusted to it, and one of his claws was wrapped in bandages, the scales on it blackened from fire.

"I'm sorry I didn't make Vermin help your claw," Shatter said as they stepped around the dead humans to pick out a bombshell.

"It's okay man, he looks like he's having a rough time of it," Blusterfew said as they lifted the bombshell together. The loading point was near the control panel, and the bombshell fitted neatly into it. Shatter gingerly pulled the lever that he saw beside it, and the loading point lifted up, up, and away. There was a satisfying click as the gears and cables that carried the bombshell into the cannon did their job.

"I've got it, Vermin, come help me aim the cannon," Sarrow said, and let go of his periscope's handles.

"Your guys seem like a pretty solid crew," Blusterfew said.

"We've come this far, I hope this isn't a mistake," Shatter replied as Sarrow and Vermin turned the wheels, and the cannon groaned above as it swiveled into position.

"You don't have too many other options, unless you want to brave the battlefield up above again," Blusterfew said.

"Cannon is in position, sir. Waiting for your command," Sarrow said.

"Very good, guys. Vermin, try to raise anyone in command, anyone at all. We'll give them a few minutes before we take our shot," Shatter said.

"Shatter, are you sure that's a good idea?" Blusterfew said.

Shatter smiled.

"There's a reason why command was trying so hard to break this fortress before whatever emergency is going on back home spooked them. Their skulking president is hiding out there, and we can end this entire war if we capture him," he said, and the other demons collectively gasped.

"Think about it. They wouldn't hide him on the Silver Isle with their gold, but the Dragon's Keep, that's a distraction. We knew they had three fledglings, so why are there only two of them at the Keep? And not only that, but remember our human pal, Charley? He wouldn't say a word about the fortress."

Vermin looked like he was going to faint.

Markus and General Gunn stormed to the shuttle, avoiding eye contact with everyone they passed. As they neared the staircase that would lead them to the basement, four soldiers stepped in front of it, blocking their path.

"Step aside, Salmone," Gunn said as he and Markus stopped. One of the soldiers, clearly a colonel by the stripes on his uniform, folded his arms insolently.

"I have orders from General Dobbs and the President to stop you from boarding the shuttle," the colonel said.

Markus tightened his grip on his mace's thick handle and looked to Gunn for reassurance, but caught only the grizzled old man's scarred eye.

"Salmone, you can't stop him from leaving," Gunn said, and put a hand out in front of Markus. "I have no desire for your stupidity to get you killed, kid, but if you and your boys don't step aside, I'm going to have to order Markus here to crack your skulls."

All four men blocking the stairs gulped, eyeing Markus and the massive, black and white mace he held warily.

Shatter jumped, startled by the crackling of the radio coming from the headset, forgotten on the ground in all the excitement. He ran for it, his heart beating as he wondered dizzily who could be contacting him. Could it be another squad, making their way to his position?

You can end the war if you pull this off, he thought, his mechanical heart beating heavily.

"...bzzt...Doomking six-six-nine, respond if alive...," said the voice through the static.

"This is Doomking six-six-nine, answering your transmission, identify, over," Shatter said as his men watched him anxiously.

"Doomking, this is Angel-Killer. I am now in charge of the Meridial *bzzt* invasion *bzzt*...that you've captured a cannon? Over," the voice on the other end asked.

"It's a general!" Shatter called to his men, and Vermin audibly gasped. "Confirm that we are currently holding onto enemy cannon, preparing to fire on enemy base, over," Shatter said into the microphone.

"Congratulations, boy, negative *bzzt*, have a small fleet at my dispos*bzzt* many cannons can you hit from your position? Over," Angel-Killer asked.

"Maybe we're not dead in the air here," Blusterfew said to Vermin, who now sat beside the remaining bombshells, watching Shatter hopefully as he gave their coordinates to the other voice over the radio.

"Not the most *bzzt* of guns to steal, but beggars like us can't be choosers! Attacking the *bzzt* would be a better option if we could take more cannons to hit it with, but *bzzt* too heavily defend *bzzt*," Angel-Killer said, but was cut off by static.

"Damn it!" Shatter said, tapping a sharp fingernail on the radio.

"New orders?" Vermin asked, and Sarrow sighed in exasperation.

"He doesn't want us to attack the fortress. Probably thinks we'll miss because he doesn't know how precise these cannons can be. I think we might have lost him though. Vermin, is there a way to get better reception with this damned thing?" Shatter said.

Before he could reply though, Shatter stiffened. His head jerked in the direction of the tunnel, and his arm began to click and shift into its sword-mode. He opened his mouth to give the order, but his men heard it as it came closer, and therefore loud enough for them to hear it. Something was coming through the tunnel.

Sarrow ran for his Soul-Scorcher, and Vermin pulled out his blasters. Blusterfew seized a rifle from the plundered weapons that had been taken off the fallen defenders of the cannon, and checked the action for ammunition.

"Take cover, Corrupters," Shatter said, and grimly smiled at Bluster.

"Guess I'm one of you now," the fiend said as he positioned himself under the console. Shatter thought it an ill omen that his friend was hiding in a place where a dead soldier had hidden, but there weren't many places to hide in the round, open cannon station. He rested his back against the wall by the tunnel entrance, and Vermin and Sarrow positioned themselves against the other walls, their weapons pointed at the tunnel's wide mouth.

The shuttle rattled its way to them, and Bluster reached for a grenade, never taking his eye off his gunsights, or his finger from the trigger as he balanced the rifle on his knee. Shatter waited, and when the shuttle came in sight, he knew, for Bluster took his shot, taking advantage of the fact that the enemy soldiers were coming in blind.

"Seven hostiles!" Sarrow yelled as he opened fire on the shouting soldiers. Shatter jammed his sword through the back of the throat of the first soldier who jumped past him, dodging Vermin's blaster fire but missing Shatter before it was too late. Blood spurted in a warm geyser, splattering Shatter's face as he screeched in fury, stepping backwards to let the dead soldier fall to the floor, his legs twitching involuntarily as his blood shot over the boots of his fellows. Vermin ran past the tunnel mouth, firing on the enemy as he went, catching one man who hadn't pulled his head down when the shooting began in the mouth. A grenade flew out of the tunnel, and Shatter launched himself at Vermin, instinctively covering the younger demon with his wings as he threw both of them against the wall where Sarrow continued to fire into the tunnel, keeping the enemy troops down. The explosion rocked the entire station, and Shatter and Vermin's heads banged together, sending the two demons staggering apart. Sarrow dropped his Soul-Scorcher, beating at his fur as flames spread across them.

"Shoot the bastards! Kill them all!" One of the soldiers hollered as they flooded the station. Shatter rolled over and blindly leaped up, shrieking as he hurtled forwards, grabbing a man by the throat as he stabbed his sword-arm through his body armor, piercing his gut. The man screamed as Shatter sank his canines into his throat, growling as they fell backwards together, warm and salty human blood filling his mouth even as it stained his uniform an uglier, darker shade that would never wash out. He heard Vermin cry out as he stabbed his sword deeper into his victim and released the squirming man. The two remaining men were running for the shuttle, and Shatter breathed in deeply, sucking in air. One of the men turned to fire a parting shot at him, and as the gas built up inside him, he threw his head back and released his fire, spewing it in a blast of red and black flame that expanded and consumed the terrified man. He lowered his head to charge after the last man, but his attention was drawn to Vermin and Sarrow, lying on the ground. Vermin held his left wrist, both of his HellsBreath blasters forgotten where he dropped them. His left hand had taken a direct shot. A grisly red hole gaped in the top of his palm, and he had lost his middle three fingers. The pink tendons and white bone hung as the fiend sat, tears flowing through his shock.

"Buddy, no," Shatter said as he knelt beside the young demon.

Sarrow stood over them, and Shatter observed his trusted corporal. The flames from the grenade had burnt most the simian demon's right side before he had put the flames out. The exposed flesh was pink, but he was covered in red burns, but still gripped his Soul-Scorcher in his right hand. Blusterfew joined them, and Shatter turned to the radio.

"Bluster, Sarrow, pile those dead husks in front of the tunnel. That'll be a good enough barricade for next time. And then try to help Vermin. I'm going to try to get the general again," Shatter ordered.

"Sir, with all due respect, I have orders to blow the tunnel if you insist on-" Salmone said, and Gunn removed his hand.

"Markus, go!" the old general growled, and the fledgling gritted his teeth and lunged forward, his wings extending menacingly as he lifted his mace for a lethal strike. White and blue energy exploded from his hands and engulfed the head of his mace as he swung at his four enemies, yelling from the exertion of his attack. The soldiers could only panic and run as the blow fell, but the discharge of power that followed

Markus smashing the colonel sent them hurtling into the stairwell, screaming as the fledgling came towards them again.

"Markus, the colonel!" General Gunn yelled, but it was too late. As Markus turned on the colonel on the floor, he was already hitting the activator.

"You son of a whore," Markus snarled.

Over a thousand pounds of TNT went off, rocking the fortress and every cannon on the battlefield with a jaw-rattling roar as the expansive tunnel system that had connected Fort Sunstrike's assets collapsed.

General Dobbs stormed past Markus, a massive pistol in his hand. The young colonel on the floor sat up, his uniform and skin burned from Markus' attack, his eyes wide with disbelief as Dobbs aimed his pistol at his forehead.

"General please, I was just doing as I was told by a superior officer-" he stammered as the General's gun went off with a deafening roar, caking the stairs with the young man's pink brain matter. The other three soldiers cowered on the floor, but the General was glaring past them.

"Come with me, boy, we've got us a moron to court martial," he growled.

"Angel-Killer, I repeat, come in, over," Shatter said, desperately trying to keep his voice level. Sarrow and Blusterfew were carrying another dead human to the pile of corpses that was blocking the tunnel.

"Angel-Killer responding, over," came the general's voice through the static once more.

"Heavy casualties, only two of us unharmed, we were attacked by a small group through the access tunnel. We've blocked the tunnel, but we can't hold the cannon without more manpower. Tell us which cannons to hit and we'll do our best, over," Shatter said.

"I don't think those husks will send any more guys over to die," Blusterfew said to Sarrow.

"They want to take their cannon back before they decide to blow it up," Sarrow replied as they lifted another body off the ground, Sarrow holding it by the head, and Blusterfew by the ankles.

"Copy that, Angel-Killer. Loading and firing the cannon is a long process, but we won't leave this station until we've hit three targets. May the spirits of the Lords of Hell watch over us all, over," Shatter said. He stood up and took the headset off.

"Alright men, new mission," Shatter said, but his words were cut off. A series of explosions began far off, the TNT in the tunnel connected to Fort Sunstrike igniting, with the charges leading up to the cannon Shatter and his squad held going like a line of fireworks. The station rocked as the tunnel collapsed, and the demons could only look to each other in panic as the TNT nearest to them went up, throwing a suffocating cloud of dirt and rock at them, blowing the barricade of corpses to bloody smithereens that spattered them with gore as they were thrown in every direction, rubble filling their lungs and eyes.

Chapter 3: The Clash of Eagles

"**N**o!" Markus screamed as he stood on the stairs, listening to the tunnel collapse.

"My boy, we need to take over operations now, or this war is completely over," Gunn said. The general holstered his pistol and stepped past the three surviving soldiers who lay on the ground still, moaning as the blue and white energy Markus had slammed them with still crackled out of their bodies. The two ran up the stairs, Markus feeling like he was in a daze as he followed the older man. The tunnel was lost. How much of it had been set off was a mystery, but if General Dobbs had collapsed the entire system, the entire defense grid of Fort Sunstrike was compromised. He imagined the demons who had captured the cannon, saw their huge, empty eyes, their yellowed, razor-sharp teeth, their horns and filthy uniforms, saw them laughing as they slaughtered and feasted on the flesh of the human soldiers of Merryland. He thought of Maria and Tolbert, and of his own parents. He would not, could not let those monsters take over Merryland, not while he drew breath.

"Markus, my boy," the general was saying as alarms sounded and they ran along a hallway, nearing the door to the command room, "I need to know that no matter what happens, you will do what's right, no matter what anyone says. The demons must be stopped at any cost, and if we've lost the tunnel systems..."

"General, I will fly out of the gates to battle them myself if it comes to that. I'm not just here to protect our simpering president, but whatever is left of our country and our people," Markus said, and the general smiled at him, a rare sight indeed.

General Gunn knocked on the door, and it was opened swiftly. A young soldier saluted him smartly and stepped aside to let him pass. A few of the techs and soldiers present saluted him as he entered, but most of them were staring at the monitors that filled the room. A few of them were crying, and General Gunn barely gave them so much of a sidelong glance as he surveyed the room.

"At ease," Gunn said as Markus followed him into the room warily.

"What's going on?" Markus demanded, but no one answered him.

"Dobbs, the boy asked a question," General Gunn barked, and General Dobbs could only look at his feet.

"Sir, with respect, the demons have fired on a cannon at the far end of the perimeter, and are preparing to fire on a second. The other cannons are requesting permission to shoot back, sir," one of the techs said, and turned back to his monitor.

"I heard them suffocate, one minute they were requesting a strike, and then the next they were screaming because the cannonball was in the air and then they were silent. The rubble pressed down on the talk button, and I had to listen to the dirt and rock falling, until their radio was crushed," another tech said in between sobs.

"Enough!" Gunn hollered. "You people are in the Meridian army, and if they destroy our cannons, their flying saucers will tear this fortress to pieces! Order the counter attack now! Bury those fucking monsters!" he commanded.

Shatter hit the fire button, and gritted his teeth as the massive gun pulled down and clicked forward above him, the report of the second cannon ball echoing like a destructive revelation throughout the station.

"They still haven't fired on us," Sarrow said as he and Blusterfew lifted the third cannonball and placed it into the loading mechanism.

"Whatever's going on up there, we've got the luck of Belial," Shatter said as he looked through one of the periscopes, and then ran back for the controls.

Trex stirred, and began coughing. The massive demon sat up, breathing heavily and staring blankly ahead. He rubbed his bullet wound, and looked blearily around the station.

"What da fuck happened while I was out?" he asked.

"Later, big luggoth," said Blusterfew, running to join Shatter. He grabbed the other wheel, and as they aimed the cannon, Vermin suddenly spoke up. He had gotten up and was standing near them, watching as they grimly prepared the final blow to the cannons of Merryland.

"Sir, I think you should evacuate the station while you can. I will stay behind to fire the cannon," he said.

"Are you out of your mind, Private?" Shatter said, and ran for the periscope again. He swiveled it around and around, licking his lips as he judged the orientation of their cannon and their target. The two cannons they had struck were both smoldering wrecks, their smoke floating into the grey sky like offerings to the fallen Lords of Hell. He saw several other cannons swiveling to face them finally, and ran for the control panel.

"With respect, sir, I think I should remain behind. The rest of you have much to live for, and..." Sarrow said, but Shatter cut him off.

"You're just trying to get a statue for your valor, but I order you to get the fuck out of here. Go make lieutenant, ape-man," Shatter said.

"Sir, I'll never fight again!" Vermin yelled, and held up his devastated hand.

Shatter replied with his own robotic hand, and nodded to the young demon.

"Trex, grab the kid and Sarrow and get the hell out of this cannon. I'm right behind you," Shatter ordered, and the huge reptilian climbed to his feet, balancing on his tail.

"I'm right behind you," Shatter said again, and hit the fire button again.

The report of the cannonball being hurled echoed once more, rattling their bones as the cannon snapped forward once more.

"Bluster, help me load another cannonball, and then get the fuck out of here," Shatter said.

"You've fired all three you promised the general," Blusterfew said.

"We need to end this. I'm going to do everything I can to break these worthless husks, but no one else needs to die," Shatter said as they both ran for the pile of cannonballs. As they lugged the fourth one to the loading mechanism, Blusterfew sighed loudly.

"Shatter, you were always a stupid hardass. You deserve a higher rank for your command, but I can't let you sacrifice yourself like this," he said.

"Don't be a worm like my men," Shatter warned.

"I'm on borrowed time already," he said as the two of them swiveled the cannon, turning their wheels to aim, "and Demon Land needs you. The world will never forgive what we will do to Merryland."

"Forget about Merryland, try what we've done to the whole world," Shatter said, and ran for the periscope. "Shit," he muttered.

"Bluster, get out of here, they're about to fire!"

"Listen to me, I know you don't care about the Empire or whatever, but listen to me, please. Your little brother, Splinter, he's a giant idiot, and he needs you. They need demons like you in the world, and think about how much harm idiots like him and your dad will do without you to say something about it," Blusterfew pressed as Shatter ran back to the controls and spun Blusterfew's wheel.

"That should do it," he said, but Blusterfew had made him think. He thought of his ridiculous brother, lusting after human girls and vampires, studying magic with an eye to joining the Spook Squad. He heard the hollow report of distant cannons, and he saluted Blusterfew, a tear brimming in his eye as the fiend ran to the periscope and then ran back, adjusting the cannon's aim as best he could.

"Hail Satan," Shatter said.

"Hail Satan," Blusterfew replied, throwing the sign of horns at his friend. Shatter spread his wings and flew for the open portal in the hill.

"Meridial's wings!" General Dobbs screamed as he watched a fourth cannonball erupt from the cannon on a monitor. Three cannonballs struck it at once, hurtling from different directions, while a fourth narrowly missed, slamming into the ground so hard that it caused a blast of dirt and rubble to scatter in every direction. The captured cannon, bent and damaged from the cannonballs, crumbled and collapsed as the shells embedded within it exploded.

"Now what?" Markus asked, looking down at his mace.

"We wait. We can still hit their saucers, even if they did take out four of our cannons," General Dobbs said. Though the mood in the room was still somber, Markus could palpably feel the relief that the threat was, for the most part, neutralized.

"Sending a man from cannon 66-B to check on the status of 43-C," one of the techs called out.

"Thank heavens Dobbs didn't blow the entire tunnel system," Gunn said.

Markus stepped out of the room and leaned against the wall, trying to catch his breath. General Dobbs, for all his confidence and bluster, had been meekly led away to await his fate in a cell. The demons would attack now, and everything depended on the compromised defense grid. If that failed and the sky urchins got too close, well, Markus would be earning the right to wield the mace of his ancient ancestor before the day was out.

Shatter screamed as the second cannonball smashed into the cannon, the collision echoing like the roar of a giant. The third cannon slammed into it from the other side, screeching as it impacted into the metal of the muzzle. Rubble and dirt were thrown into the air, and Shatter tried to gesture as he opened his mouth to issue an order, but then the cannonballs embedded in the severely damaged cannon went off in succession, shaking the earth as the tons of steel machinery within the cannon sundered apart, severely damaged from the three explosions that had gone off within it. The superstructure of the station collapsed within, and dirt and concrete erupted in all directions as the cannon crumbled. Trex roared and leapt behind Shatter, spreading his arms wide as he stood as tall as he could.

"Get down!" Shatter screamed as Vermin and Sarrow watched the apocalyptic cloud of destructing flooding towards them, jaws agape in horror. Shatter dove into them, bowling the three of them down at Trex's feet as the shadow of the rubble cascaded over them. They were engulfed as the reptilian demon bellowed from the pain, hunching over his three comrades. There was no stopping the dust and dirt as it struck them, filling their nostrils and eyes, bruising them with bricks and chunks of metal. A fourth cannonball went off, throwing dirt and rocks on the far side of the hill, and when the noise was nothing more than the ghost of an echo ringing in their ears, Shatter opened his eyes to find that his wings were wrapped tightly around his body. Trex fell forward, groaning hideously, and Sarrow tried to catch him in vain. The reptilian was too massive, and Trex, unable to stop his fall, knocked the simian demon out of his way as he collapsed to the ground. The back of Trex's uniform was torn to pieces, and his spines and scales glinted in the silvery moonlight.

"I won't rest until that beast gets a heroic discharge," Shatter said as Vermin and Sarrow arose, shaking from the trauma of what they had just experienced.

"We need to get to the truck," Sarrow muttered.

The Corrupters ran along the ravaged hill, desperate to reach their stolen truck. Not a single one of them believed that the barrage was finished as the destroyed cannon still went through its death throes above them. The metal fell and whined as it was bent by falling plaster and stone, and Shatter hoped that for his pal Blusterfew, the end had been painless.

The truck was gone. Where it was wasn't even a question on their minds as they stared agape at the blasted hill as the grass around the impact crater burned, the flames dying even as they stood there, the hope hopped up on adrenaline they had in their hearts fading along with them. They had seen the annihilating power of those cannonballs before, but had never been so close to an impact zone before, even though they had spent close to a month in this warzone.

"Well then, I guess it's time to find a trench," Sarrow the Chin said.

"Too bad we left our supply pack in the cannon with Bluster," Shatter said, looking wistfully at one of the distant cannon-hilltops. Something within it still burned from where they had struck it with one of their own cannonballs, sending smoke to join the black herd of smoke clouds that rolled above them, chasing the silver of the moon. Shatter looked to the beautiful full moon, its unholy, silver light shining despite the smoke and dust their cannon had thrown at it, and tried to breathe deeply, though gunfire and explosions punctured the serenity of the beautiful darkness.

"Guess it's back to the trenches," Vermin muttered sourly.

"The other cannons are all turning," Sarrow observed. It was true. They well all turning to the north of where the Corrupters were facing. And then, through the fog of war came the fleet of sky urchins. There were four of them, humming as their two halves spun, the scarlet lights on their spinning spikes tracing bloody halos in the darkness as they swerved gracefully through the air, dodging the cannonballs that were flying at them. The radio Vermin had forgotten he was holding suddenly crackled with static, and Shatter grabbed the headset that was dragging by its wire.

"This is Ghoulking eight-nine-nine, I repeat, this is Ghoulking eight-nine-nine, over," Shatter said.

"Congratulations on making captain, Ghoulking, we see you on our scanners, I'll be picking you up for the final assault on those husk bastards," Angel-Killer crackled in his ear.

"Just a little longer, boys, that's our ride back there," he said his voice breaking with emotion, and reached for Vermin's damaged hand. "You're gonna be okay, buddy, all of us are."

The wind blew, and Shatter took a deep breath as he closed his eyes, listening to the whine of the sky urchins' engines, the whistle of cannonballs whizzing past them harmlessly to explode elsewhere, ending more lives and punching craters in the ground, and the screech of some missile hurtling through the air.

He opened his eyes, and was startled to see all three of his fellow Ghoul Troopers staring past him, their mouths hanging open. Even Trex had his toothy croc maw dangling, drool pooling on his boots as it dripped from his yellowed fangs and tongue.

"You guys okay?" Shatter asked, tapping his Soul-Scorcher.

Vermin merely pointed, and Shatter turned around in time to see a black and blue blur ripping through the sky, streaking directly for the sky urchin that was headed towards them. There was an eruption of white light that blinded them all with its radiance as it struck the side of the tremendous flying saucer, and the sky urchin seemed to stay where it was for a second, hanging in the air as the trauma to its side reverberated through it, shaking every nut and bolt as the two interlocked halves of the craft continued to spin, screeching as electronic components and fuel deposits, ignited by a mystical explosion that had rocked the sky urchin, failed and went up in flames.

"I...think our ride just crashed," Sarrow said, unable to tear his eyes away from the sky urchin as it fell to the erde, churning the dirt as it plunged through a hill, devastating the cannon perched atop it. An ophidia andiron, buried in debris, was unearthed and thrown sky-high by the momentum of the fallen craft, and when it finally hit the ground again, its crash was drowned out by the shot of another cannon, taking a pot-shot at one of the remaining sky urchins. It dodged, swerving down so that the cannonball flew harmlessly past it.

"There," Shatter said, pointing at a glowing speck that was fluttering near the sky urchins. He glanced behind him, and his heart sank. He had forgotten how badly hurt Trex was.

"I could probably make the shot," Vermin said doubtfully as he and Sarrow eyed the reptilian's sniper rifle. Shatter opened his mouth to reply, but he was startled by the nearest sky urchin as it fired a barrage of missiles at its assailant. The glowing speck dropped out of the sky, diving away as the missiles screeched towards it, before flying back towards the cluster of sky urchins, its light expanding again as it streaked back upwards.

"It wasn't running, it was building up power," Sarrow said.

The light expanded outwards like a neutron star exploding, detonating every missile that was attempting to follow it. As flaming chunks of metal rained from the sky, the white-blue speck became a blur once more, aimed at the sky urchin that had just unsuccessfully fired on it.

"It's one of their fledglings," Shatter said as he began running down the hill.

"I think you might be right if they're breaking out one of their angel-whelps. That fortress is hiding the husk president," Vermin said, following Shatter.

The sky urchin spun gracefully, its mechanical parts roaring like thunder as the spiked saucer turned nearly completely vertically, just barely avoiding being struck by the nemesis that had felled the first ship.

"Fuck!" Shatter screamed as a cannonball directly struck the craft as it hummed out of control. The cannonball hurtled through the urchin, the BOOM! of the impact and the busted metal making the chiropteran demon screech in pain. A vision of the hands onboard the doomed craft flooded his mind as it plummeted.

"Sarrow, you're in command. Keep these scum dogs alive until I get back," Shatter ordered, and spread his wings.

"Lieutenant!" Vermin yelled, but with a running leap and a few beats of his great, black, leathery wings, Shatter was airborne, his cybernetic arm swiftly shifting into its sword-mode.

Shatter flew into the air as if nothing had ever been holding him down. When they had initially invaded Eggshank, he had witnessed Locusts falling from the sky, blackened from thunder tank fire, or stricken dead by sniper bullets. Flight on his part was restricted to close combat. Shatter remembered well his father's reaction to his son's decision to enlist. Senator Malekarm was a shrewd strategist in all areas of life, and never let any asset go spinning off without his touch to set it in a direction that benefited him. This included his three sons, and while Void had spurned their father's interest, Shatter and Splinter looked up to their father.

"The Grand Army of Apollyon is what makes all this possible," Malekarm had said.

They were walking through the lush garden behind their mansion. Purple nightshade flowers and lavender roses lolled all around them in the soothing summer wind of that night, and they walked a path marked by black flagstones that shimmered in the moonlight.

"They can teach me to be strong, like Grandfather Isaiah. Wanderous has been talking to the recruiter, and Edge is thinking about joining too," Shatter said, trying to meet his father's eyes, but the elder statesman kept his eyes focused ahead. They were ambling, in an indirect and casual pathway, towards the center of the garden. There a lavish marble fountain stood, its water flowing upwards in a graceful arc that spilled outwards into a mossy pond from which the fountain arose like an otherworldly white tree. Within the bowl of the fountain was an obsidian globe of Erde, turning slowly as the water churned beneath it.

"Absalom's cup runneth over," Malekarm said, invoking the name of the eternal emperor of Demon Land as they drew closer to the fountain.

"I wouldn't enlist until I graduated, and I'm not completely sure I want to do it," Shatter said, keeping step with his father as the Senator walked off the path.

"Did you have any other prospects?" Malekarm asked, the batwings folded over his body rising gently as he sighed.

"I was thinking about joining the Moonrise Guild," Shatter said as he tried to step away from the direction his father was leading him in. His father gave him a sidelong glance as he followed Shatter, and the young chiropteran felt a petty joy in not being led towards the fountain again.

"That vampire haven? That is a dead end, boy, and you know it," Malekarm said dismissively, and he finally met his son's eyes. Malekarm's eyes were perfectly black pools in his face that seemed to sink into infinity, and his beard was overgrown and long, yet carefully trimmed so that it did not cover his small, clever mouth. The fur that covered his scales was slightly reddish in contrast with his black beard, and the tufts of hair sticking out of his tall bat ears was like ghostly-white smoke.

"I only brought it up because I want to visit the moon someday," Shatter said, looking up at the meteor-scarred face of the silver moon.

"Let the vampires waste their eternal, blood-guzzling nights on perfecting space travel. I don't need my son dying because a heat shield wasn't properly placed," Malekarm said.

"Well, I'm probably going to enlist with the Locusts. I can bring glory-," Shatter started to say, but his father cut him off.

"You cannot enlist with the Locusts, they are the first to fly in, the first to die," the Senator said dismissively, and Shatter realized, too late that they were once again walking towards the fountain.

"But dad, I'm chiropteran, we can fly better than any bird, any bug. I can be a mighty fighter, just like Isaiah! Imagine how fast I can be promoted! I can be an admiral someday!" Shatter pressed.

"Splinter will be a powerful sorcerer one day, and I shall be Chancellor, once we've dealt with the Over-Seer. With enough prodding, Void will take up our family's earldom when your uncle sunders. You should not be wasted on the off-chance you survive a Meridial flak gun or thunder tank." They stopped before the fountain, and the Senator gestured towards it. "That globe is our birthright, the prize of all demonkind. Someday we will prize what remains of Erde from our enemies overseas, and this entire planet will toil beneath our whip. Let the vampires float around in outer space, and let the avians and bugs clear the way for our sky urchins to dominate the skies. Our ancestor, Isaiah, slew the Arch-Angel Gabrielle. I will not see my son wasted when he can be commanding a sky urchin of his own, or directing legions of Ghoul Troopers as a general or knight," Malekarm said, and though he turned to his son, Shatter's sullen eyes did not turn away from the sleek, glossy black surface of the obsidian globe of Erde as the waters relentlessly tossed it within the fountain, turning it over and over endlessly so that none of its etched continents were safe from drowning.

That conversation was the first and last word his father gave on Shatter's choices. He enlisted with the Ghoul Troopers, and it wasn't long after the bombardment and invasion of Eggshank that he made lieutenant, and was given his own command. He glanced wistfully at their squad's name, painted on each of their chests below the sigil of Apollyon by Vermin. The farm boy had spelled "Corrupters" wrong, but after everything they had endured on their campaign to break Fort Sunstrike, he resolved to never allow the mistake to be corrected. They would remain Shatter Howler's Corrupters forever, in history, song, and film.

He rose through the crisp night, feeling like he had been sleeping for the entire duration of the war as he caught a current and flew like a kite, his flapping wings effortlessly carrying him higher and higher. A cannonball, fired from a distant cannon, whistled through the air, and he watched as it missed one of the last two sky urchins, slamming into the ground far, far away. His sensitive ears heard the clamor of warfare far below, screams and gunfire ravaging the tranquility of the night. Soul-Scorchers discharged, and when he looked down, flapping his wings as he drew closer and closer to the embattled sky urchins, he saw the tell-tale fire-orange beams of Soul-Scorchers leaping across the battlefield, and heard a human begging for their life as a demon screamed in savage triumph.

He saw the fledgling as he flew for another sky urchin, easily dodging another salvo of missiles with a few powerful beats of his beautiful black wings. The blue and white light began to emanate from his body again, and Shatter glided above him like a shadow cast by the moon. The fledgling was just a boy, his long black hair streaming behind him as he built up his angelic power for a strike. The sky urchin tore past them, roaring as it obscured the boy, and Shatter dropped down to the boy's level, flapping his leathery wings harder as the fledgling pursued his massive foe like a bird of prey. Shatter breathed deeply and screeched as loudly as he could, the muscles in his throat stretching painfully as his voice, high-pitched and jarring at its weakest, was aimed directly at his quarry. The light that surrounded the boy flickered as was struck by the sound of Shatter's voice, and as Shatter flew past him, the boy threw him a shocked, agonized look. The knuckles of the hand that held his mace looked ready to burst, and Shatter gave him an evil smile as he turned in mid-air. He tumbled backwards as he screeched again, his lungs burning. The boy flew drunkenly towards Shatter, and a cannonball whistled past them as the demon turned and regained his form, flapping away from the pursuing fledgling.

Guess that got the brat's attention, the demon thought happily as the second sky urchin hummed past them overhead.

He abruptly changed direction and flew towards his foe, who could not react quickly enough as Shatter stabbed his sword-arm forward, piercing the boy in his side right through his bulletproof fatigues. He swung his legs up and kicked him in the chest with his boots, pushing the helpless fledgling off his sword as he swung his mace, too slowly. Shatter fluttered away as the boy roared in frustration, catching himself as he fell, blood falling through the night from his stab wound. Shatter came up behind him, but Markus blocked the demon's swing with his mace, saving his neck from a killing stroke. Shatter grinned as vibrations ran up his sword-arm, and pulled away as Marcus beat his massive wings, climbing higher as energy began to build up in his body once more. The wind buffeted Shatter as he tucked in his wings to drop away. But Markus came for him, the air crackling with latent power as he grasped his mace with both hands over his head. Shatter was too agile for the fledgling, and spun away, shrieking gleefully. Cannons were firing! Smoke and steam rose from the battlefield below, and the dead and dying groaned as explosions rocked artillery and shattered bodies in the midst of panic or sleep. Shatter reveled in his power, flying around Markus as the boy swung for him again, energy and light flashing like lightning that blinded Shatter even as he dodged his attacks with ease.

He tried to call out to Markus, but the wind from a cannonball drowned his voice out.

Screw it, Shatter thought, and drew in another deep breath. Markus shouted and hurtled towards his foe, but he wasn't expecting Shatter to spew a blast of fire out of his maw. The flames reflected off of his dark eyes, and Markus brought the massive, spiked head of his mace up just in time to block the fire blast. He screamed as the flames burst around his weapon, scorching his hair. Embers broke against his mace's spikes, burning his forehead and eyes, and he shot upwards, desperate to escape from the demon's fire.

He breathed deeply, beating at the flames that were burning in his long hair. The demon was nowhere beneath him, and Markus looked over his shoulder in a panic, but it was too late. He heard the fluttering of the wings before he felt the demon's sword-arm hack at his right wing.

"Nothing personal, angel-boy," Shatter whispered in Markus's ear as he wrapped his free claw around the fledgling's mace and sawed at his wing, breaking the delicate bones and splattering his uniform with blood as he swerved away. Markus screamed in terror as he fell, black feathers trailing him as he pathetically flapped his wings in vain. Shatter watched him fall, his arm shifting out of its sword mode.

Shatter flew after the last two sky urchins, looking wistfully in the direction of the destroyed cannon where he had left his troop behind. The mace buzzed in his hands, but did not directly threaten him. He breathed deeply, his head swimming. Just like the day he had enlisted, this day was the end of a paradigm. Nothing would ever be the same for any of the Corrupters if they survived this battle. He gripped the stolen mace tightly with both hands, cybernetic and organic, wondering how Vermin would choose to deal with his ruined hand. Would he take a Heroic Discharge, and keep his natural hand? Or would he accept a cybernetic upgrade? Would he give up his entire forearm, as Shatter had done? Cybernetic upgrades were an expectation when a demon enlisted with as a Ghoul Trooper. The fact that he was the only one in his squad with any upgrades was simply a testament to how green they were.

He thought about Blusterfew's words, the words that had convinced to him to make the snap decision to let his friend sacrifice himself. Splinter was an idiot, and he was an entitled little brat to boot as well. When Shatter got out of his tour of duty though, he would be able to keep an eye on him, as well as their father. The Senator was ambitious and crafty, and Shatter knew that someday, there might be no one left to stand between him and his designs on the empire's future. An eruption ripped the demon from his thoughts as a cannon fired on one of the sky urchins. It swerved away, dodging the cannonball, only to be fired on by at least two other cannons. The other sky urchin spun higher above, hurtling towards the fortress, only to be chased away by several cannonballs as well. They made progress, but slowly, too slowly. As they drew closer, Shatter saw that mounted on the fortress was a battery of heavy artillery guns. They were trained on the two sky urchins as they hummed and spun out of the crisscrossing trajectories of cannonballs, and even a blast from a thunder tank, tearing through the smog and smoke of war. The guns were not manned, but as they swiveled and moved up and down, keeping their barrels tightly pointed at the urchins, Shatter was sure they were not automated. Someone was clearly controlling them from deep inside the fortress.

Shatter sped towards them, wincing as one of the sky urchins fired a salvo of missiles at one of the cannons. A blast of flak burst up from far down, detonating the missiles as they sped towards their target, and Shatter silently thanked the Lords of Hell that he was not the target of the black flak cloud. He would have been shredded in an instant, not even a drizzle of blood left of him.

A cannonball aimed at one of the urchins missed as it zoomed upwards, but slammed full-on into the other as it descended, speeding towards the fortress. The blow sent a shockwave through the air that made every molecule of ash and water in the air tremble. Shatter shrieked in dismay, turning to watch as the stricken sky urchin spun crazily towards Fort Sunstrike, its missiles exploding from its sides as it made its approach. It wobbled as smoke and sparks shot out of its damaged hull, and the battery of guns locked onto it, their rotors whining as their multiple barrels spun, shooting lead death at the doomed warship. Several missiles struck home, blasting holes in the concrete walls of the fortress, enveloping its filthy banners in orange flames that lit the night in gaudy defiance, but most of them were struck by gunfire, detonating mid-air. Almost like a capstone to a metal concert, the cannonball that was lodged in the sky urchin exploded, killing the crew and sending the warship spinning off blindly into the night. As Shatter landed on the roof of the fortress, the dead sky urchin howled over him, trailing broken pieces as it spent its momentum on its fall.

The other guns turned their attention on the final sky urchin as it hovered above a cannon, the very cannon that had just felled the other sky urchin. Bodies littered the rooftop, the remains of several failed raids on the fortress to judge from the various states of decomposition Shatter could see as he ran towards the guns. Some of the bodies were blasted in half, their rotting guts hanging from their torsos, while others were not so lucky. One demon, a simian-fiend mix from the look of his decomposing face, still clutched his HellsBreath blaster in one claw. His other claw was gone, blasted off months ago by one of the huge guns that served as the last line of defense for Fort Sunstrike. Shatter thought of the crew in the downed sky urchin, imagined the navigator gripping the controls, desperate to make his impending death mean something as he aimed the crashing warship at the fortress. Like all of the brave, dead demonic soldiers that littered the roof, it had come to nothing. Shatter breathed in deeply, his stolen mace held high. Fire spewed from deep within him, turning the gun red hot as the orange-black flames spiraled out of his body and engulfed the line of guns. With a savage grunt, he swung his stolen mace at the first gun, denting the barrels and breaking the rotor assembly. The mace seemed to awaken from this assault, and sparked to life, shining with a white light from within as it vibrated in Shatter's claws. He swung it once more, and the gun snapped clean off its mount, flying off into the night as the gears within continued to turn. He ran for the next gun, and as he swung the angelic weapon, he felt its power flow into him, strengthening the blow he dealt to the gun. Metal shards erupted like a meteor shower, and the flames that billowed from him were empowered by the magic mace, the white energy infused in the stream of orange Hellfire that he breathed on the next gun in line. The other guns that were installed along the perimeter of the fortress's roof were turning to face him, but he was too swift for them. Like a shadow he tore through them, fire and angelic light bursting from him as he snarled and shattered the defenses of his foes. He thought of Blusterfew, buried under the rubble of the cannon, firing one last cannonball off; Vermin taking a bullet in one of his healer's hands; Trex shot in the head, and holding back the debris of the cannon with nothing but his body; Sarrow burned and battered, barely alive; the crews of every fallen sky urchin; the countless other demons that had been incinerated by the ranks of thunder tanks that defended Eggshank to the bitter end; and of his father and two brothers back home, in the megacity of Duskrim. Not far from the fortress, the final sky urchin stopped above a cannon. Its lower compartment opened like a malevolent rose, the panels sliding out like sharp petals as its tractor beam fired downwards in a pillar of indigo light with a hiss. Shatter screeched in triumph as the cannon was torn from the ground, the station and firing apparatus torn from the erde with a crunch that reverberated like a gunshot. He saw the soldiers that had been stationed in the cannon, suspended in the blue beam like helpless ants as the station broke apart, the debris and humans hanging for one, fateful second. And then the beam went out, and it all fell back down, crashing back into the black hole in the ground it had been ripped from. Shatter heard the helpless soldiers' terrified screams as they fell, but they were stifled by countless tons of twisted metal and stone.

The sky urchin spun towards the fortress now, unopposed as Shatter went to work on the last three guns. As it hovered above him, blotting out the moon, the bottom compartment opened once more, and the demon looked up in time to see a higher compartment within the warship open as the tractor beam came to life again. The crew of the sky urchin descended within the beam, and Shatter growled as he broke the last gun.

Chapter 4: The Phalanx

Shatter saluted the admiral as he descended with his troop in the tractor beam.

"At ease, Captain," the admiral said as his boots touched the roof and the tractor beam switched off, and he saluted Shatter back. His uniform was like Shatter's, but the sash over his shoulder was a deep maroon, indicating his rank. He held his helmet under his left arm, and had a Soul-Scorcher strapped to his back, just as every one of his soldiers had. He looked around at the old death and gore that littered the rooftop, a perfect microcosm of the battlefield. Another demon joined him at his side. Dressed like any Ghoul Trooper, he had a long scabbard buckled to his belt, as well as what looked like two human-style projectile pistols, one holstered on either side of his hip. This demon was partially insectoid and partially something else, with a large, round head that was covered in yellow fur, and green compound eyes that shimmered with the morbid light of distant fire. His mouth was wide and filled with sharp teeth, and four translucent wings buzzed on his back like a chainsaw. He walked away from his small group of soldiers and knelt before one of the demonic corpses and gently closed his eyes, and pushed the unfortunate's jaws closed.

"If only I had the time to close the eyes of every fallen brave, I would console every grieving mother. Alas, no peace in life for demonkind, no peace in death," the demon said morosely.

"I am Admiral Warth, and that poetic fool is Sir Gall Heranomous, our resident knight. Where is the rest of your squad?" the admiral asked Shatter as two other soldiers responded to a gesture from him and moved to set up charges as the rest stood far away from them, patiently waiting as they hooked up wires and prepared for their final assault on the fortress.

"I was forced to leave them behind to save what was left of our fleet when I saw the fledgling," he said, and his eyes roved out into the darkness.

The admiral stood beside him, watching as blood-red Soul-Scorcher rays and flames flared out on the field of battle through the night like welts in the darkness.

"This assault will be the end of the war," the admiral said.

"I know. I figured they had their president skulking behind all these fucking cannons," Shatter said bitterly.

"You've lost friends, boy, but every soldier I see dying out there, every transmission that is cut off too short, every loss we sustain, is a trajectory towards glory that I have failed in. As a commander, I want not only to achieve the aims and ambitions of the empire, but also to raise every one of my boys as high as I can. Whenever I lose one, it's a personal loss. This is the agony of command, a responsibility you share with me. When this nightmare is over, your Corrupters will be vaster than before, and I pray to the memory of Great Satan that you feel a fraction of the grief I feel now, standing on this rooftop, on the cusp of our triumph, surrounded by the mutilated bodies of so many brave young men," Admiral Warth said.

"Is Sir Gall under your command?" Shatter asked.

"He is not. Knights ride along with any troop they wish to, and while they take orders from the commanding officer, they do not have to follow them if they don't wish to. Gall's entire life is a never-ending soliloquy, and everyone within earshot of him is his captive audience. I try not to pay him any heed as he shows off. Damn good fighter though," Warth said. One of the soldiers setting up charges gestured to the admiral, and he nodded.

"Prepare for detonation!" he yelled.

The rooftop was massive, and Sir Gall came to join Shatter and the Admiral by the edge as the technicians took up their positions and waited for the admiral's signal.

"You're with me, Captain Shatter," Gall said, grinning at Shatter.

Shatter looked to Admiral Warth, but the admiral was busy watching his technicians as he nodded to them to fire.

"You might think I'm a fool, but I can show you a thing or two once we get down there," Gall said.

"I said nothing of the sort," Shatter protested, but the knight tapped his temple with a smirk.

"I can hear those callous thoughts swimming on the surface of your weary little mind," Gall said, and he chuckled as understanding dawned on Shatter's face.

"So, you're psychic then? You can read minds?" Shatter asked incredulously.

The explosives went off, throwing plaster and masonry into the air.

"No time for chit-chat, if you're taking Captain Shatter, you better not lose him, or I'll follow you into Hell and torment your essence myself," Warth said, and stormed off to his waiting legion.

"Shall we then?" Sir Gall asked, and spun around with a beckoning gesture to Shatter. Gall stepped off the edge of the hole in the roof with a grace that was ethereal, falling into the bright hole below as he drew his sword from the sheath at his side. Shatter followed him, wishing to Satan's memory that he could be getting orders from the admiral with the rest of the soldiers as he spread his wings and dropped down behind the knight, his arm shifting into its sword-mode.

They stood in a room that had no personnel to speak of, but was full of stacks of crates, several of which were cracked open, showing the heavy guns that were stored within. Gall tried to open the door, but it was locked, and so kicked it off its hinges with a single savage blow of his boot.

"That thing handle?" Gall asked as Shatter stabbed through the control panel for a set of double doors blocking a staircase.

"It handles perfectly for what I need it to do, mostly slitting throats and wrecking machinery like this," Shatter replied as he pulled his sword-arm out of the ruined screen. The knight kicked the doors open, smirking at Shatter as he followed him down the stairs.

"All you Ghoul Troopers are the same, following orders until they lead you to your grave. Stand in formation, shoot those husks, execute that governor, march in the rain, rip out your eyeballs, torch that city, massacre those innocents, chop off your arm! Don't worry, it'll be great, you'll get medals, an entire fucking parade in exchange for your blood, sweat, and soul!" Gall said, and came to a stop at the landing. Through the thick glass windows of the doors he could see two soldiers watching them, their rifles trained on them. Soldiers lined the hallway, all of them anxiously looking over their commanders' shoulders at the demonic interlopers.

Shatter set his mace down and was unshouldering his Soul-Scorcher, but the knight gave him a dismissive gesture.

"Don't bother, young ghoul. I'm going to cut those husks to ribbons so fast they won't even be able to aim their ridiculous guns at us," Gall said.

Shatter shook his head and jammed his sword-arm into the door's control panel.

"If you think you can keep up, feel free to show us how that sword-arm handles!" Gall said as he kicked the doors open and launched himself into the hallway. Gunfire and screaming followed, and Shatter cautiously peered into the hall in time to see Gall springing from one soldier to the next, severing their heads as they futilely aimed their guns at him, terror in their eyes at the grinning, bug-eyed demonic knight. Shatter followed casually, a steady torrent of blood from a headless soldier's corpse spraying over his boots as he followed in the knight's wake.

"What think you, Captain? Should we pursue these helpless villains?" Gall asked, his wings buzzing happily as he wiped blood off his sword's blade with one of his gloved claws.

"You sure they aren't bringing reinforcements?" Shatter asked, his arm shifting out of its sword-mode.

"They had nothing but panic and self-preservation on their minds," Gall replied.

"And just what do you think is on my mind?" Shatter demanded.

"I'm a little surprised at how bored you are, unless you're just trying to mask your thoughts, but really, I don't need you to like me. I'm doing you a favor, counting you in on this victory. You wanna get from lieutenant to general for winning this war? That might happen, kid," Gall said as Shatter caught up to him.

"I think you've got the wrong idea of me," the chiropteran said, and stopped guarding his mind. Gall's smirk evaporated as Shatter's arm shifted back to its sword-mode. Gall blocked Shatter's blow with a casual swing of his sword, but psychic or not, was unprepared for Shatter to headbutt him in the face, knocking him backwards.

"That was most...unbecoming of a warrior," Gall said, rubbing his head as he stepped backwards.

"Disrespect me again, and you'll see how 'unbecoming' a Ghoul Trooper can be," Shatter said, rubbing his own head as he went past the knight to reclaim his mace, spitting on the knight's boots.

Gall nearly said something about showing your back to your foes, but then thought better about it. He would get what he wanted out of the young captain after all was said and done, after all.

The hallway led to a wide, well-lit atrium that led to more hallways still. A company of soldiers waited there, and Shatter could see the three soldiers that had fled the slaughter of their squad standing near the rear of the formation, the blood of their fellow husks staining their green fatigues.

"Demons, stop! We will accept your surrender if you back away," the sergeant in the front yelled.

The two of them stopped, and Shatter looked to the knight.

"How quickly you've learned to communicate with me, if only you could read my mind," Gall said. "But this is no narrow hallway, those husk bastards will shoot us a trillion times over. Best get that gun off your back," Gall said, and lowered his sword.

"Any chance you'll let us pass so we can go kill your weak president and take over your worthless country?" Gall asked as Shatter's arm shifted back and he unslung his Soul-Scorcher.

"Your soldiers are getting slaughtered throughout this fortress," the sergeant said, and raised his hand. The thirty-odd soldiers flicked their safeties off and aimed their guns at the insectoid knight.

"If you're so certain of victory, why not open fire and just put me down?" Gall asked.

"If it's all the same to you," the sergeant said, and glanced at one of the blood-spattered soldiers, "I'd like to survive this day rather than risking a skirmish with two soldiers that have already killed a squadron all to their selves. Besides, it isn't like you two maggots stand a chance of winning this, no matter how many of us you kill. You might not be human, but you've got feelings, some drive to survive, don't you?" the sergeant asked.

"I see why you're just a lowly sergeant," Gall said as Shatter's Soul-Scorcher's ray fired over his shoulder, scorching the sergeant's face into a sizzling red mass of blackened flesh. The other soldiers recoiled and began firing, but Gall had been ready for them, pirouetting backwards as Shatter's hateful red ray strafed across the atrium, striking the men in their chests and legs as he lowered the gun and retreated back into the hallway as the hailstorm of bullets turned towards him. He could hear Gall's terrible laughter over the sound of bullets imbedding themselves in the plaster of the walls, the men yelling orders at one another, the copper shells hitting the floor. There were many in the modern age that believed swords were obsolete in the face of projectile and demonic-essence based beam weaponry, Shatter reflected as he ran into the atrium, taking a human through the heart as he stabbed through his fatigues, growling as the man's blue eyes drowned in Shatter's empty, black orbs before his face was destroyed by the huge mace in his left claw. Splinter, Shatter's little brother, had been one such demon when their father had decreed that his youngest would be a swordsman. In truth, Shatter had agreed with his brother. It wasn't as if his bionic arm was his main weapon, especially not when he had a troop of demonic warriors at his side, all with their own enhancements. However, watching Gall work certainly put him in a different state of mind. The demon knight had footwork that would make a fugue dancer quake with jealousy, and his lithe form moved with a delicacy that would never translate to the war movie they would make of this day. Shatter's own agonized steel sword-arm was made for close-combat killing, and as he hacked one soldier's machine gun in half and stabbed another through the mouth, punching his front teeth down his throat with a crunch like cracking porcelain, he spat his foes' blood back at them with a delirious laugh. He never regretted trading in his organic arm for this, especially not while the angelic mace enhanced his strength.

"Please," the last soldier sobbed as Shatter kicked him in the head, breathing in deeply. Behind him he could hear Gall's deep breathing as he sidestepped and closed in on his last two enemies. There was more art to his fighting style than an over-reliance on his sword, a dependence and a trust in his footwork. He was instinctively measuring his breathing, keeping his attention on the foe with the highest chance of shooting him. When his sword struck, it always struck true. These human soldiers were trained to aim and shoot at their targets until they were dead, maybe pull a knife if necessary. There was precious little they could do to a foe who refused to give them the space to adapt as he distracted them and then dodged to get closer in order to sever their heads. Shatter turned from his enemy as he rolled on the ground, burning with orange-black flames that clung and refused to die. He had headbutted the knight, but only because the knight had fully expected him to sword fight him, demon-to-demon. He would never get such a chance again, now that the knight knew what kind of fighter he was, psychic abilities or no. Shatter focused his ensorcered eyes on the ceiling above, peering through the masonry as best he could to get a view on what awaited them.

"Don't bother, Captain," Gall said as he stepped out of his final soldier's line of fire and sliced the boy's hand clean off, making him drop his weapon with a shocked scream.

"The president is this way," Gall said, tapping his temple as he went down one of the three yawning hallways. Shatter took a final look at the carnage they were leaving behind. Headless men splattered blood across a tiled floor that was flecked with blood and bodies. Guns with severed hands still gripping them lay abandoned, and heads stared forlornly where they had fallen, mouths and eyes wide in disbelief at their own deaths. The boy Shatter had doused in his own Hellfire was dead, his body still smoldering. Vermin had a camera, and for the first time since his deployment, Shatter wished he had one of his own. Here was a microcosm of the barbarism his kind perpetrated against the self-righteous, dead-angel-worshipping husks of Merryland. Did these frail mortals really pose a threat to the dominance of Demon Land?

Gall stood before a heavy steel door, patiently waiting for Shatter. Fighting was going on all throughout the fortress, and Shatter focused his ears on the door.

"Your natural gift is like a low-rank version of my mind-reading," said Gall.

"That's funny, because I can hear everything, while you can only read what I let you," Shatter retorted, and breathed in deeply.

"Save your breath," the knight said, and reached into his gilded tunic. He produced what looked like a ball of silver string.

"Whatever that is, why reveal it now, after I've stabbed through every electric lock?" Shatter demanded.

"Because this door doesn't have an electric lock," Gall said, and tapped his temple with a smirk. He held the ball out, and the string began to unspool itself, sliding into the doorjamb and into the door's locking mechanism. The people inside the room began to argue within, and Shatter looked down at his red-stained sword-arm as the door unlocked, and slid open. The string returned Gall's palm, wrapping back into a ball.

"Nifty toy, my honorable sir," Shatter said as the knight kicked the door open.

"Every job has a different tool, it's not all sword-swinging," Gall replied with a wink.

The control room was lit by a florescent array on the ceiling that flickered every time a grenade went off on the floors above them, plunging the room into brief darkness, lit only by the buzzing computer screens that littered the desktops all over the room. A dozen or so technicians stared at the two demonic soldiers as they stepped into the room, covered in gore and brandishing their weapons as they took in the room. There were a couple of soldiers, but these looked towards a grizzled, one-eyed general who stood quietly, observing the invaders gracefully.

"It's over! Surrender your weapons and lay on the ground!" Shatter ordered. The technicians, petrified, complied, but the soldiers continued to look to their commander, their weapons held uncertainly.

The general motioned for his men to lower their weapons, never taking his eye off of Shatter. The men obeyed, trembling as they maintained their positions.

"You're the little bastard that screeched in my ear, aren't you?" General Gunn asked Shatter.

"The very same one who broke your cannon array and killed your little angel boy," Shatter hissed, looking from one face to the next.

"Where's your fucking president? We need him," he added.

The general was silent, solemnly gazing at the two demons standing amidst his broken command center with his one good eye. Shatter could see through the old man's closed eyelid, could see the empty socket; did the humans not have bionic eyes? Did this old man, marked by his life of warfare and command, choose not to install a weapon in that ancient wound?

"You think too deeply," Gall said, and barred his teeth at one of the technicians at her computer. "Surrender your president and we might just leave here without harming any of you. We want this war over as much as you do." The technician recoiled, her blue eyes wide with terror.

"Alien and hideous? You've never seen a fly up close? Never seen the scaly skin of a fiend?" Gall flicked his forked tongue at the female and turned his attention back to the general.

The tumult of warfare raged all around them now; Shatter heard demons screaming, barking orders, and laughing, while humans did the same. Gunfire, bullets slamming into plaster and bone, beams of concentrated demonic-essence ending lives. Fires burned. Furniture and doors were destroyed, glass shattered, bones cracked and skin broken.

The general opened his mouth to speak, but Gall was smirking more hideously than he had the entire incursion.

"Did he just think about the location of a goldmine?" Shatter asked, but the question answered itself immediately. A man in a wrinkled pink button-up shirt and black dress pants emerged from under one of the desks that was facing the general and his soldiers.

"You knew where he was this entire time, didn't you?" Shatter asked.

"Just wanted to see if he was really as cowardly as we believed," the knight replied, and extended his blade to the quaking man's throat. The soldiers were looking in disbelief at the two demons, as if they were just beginning to realize just how fucked they were. The Soul-Scorchers were getting louder as the invading force drew ever closer, and their president was exposed, unable to flee. A sky urchin spun above their fortress, ready to destroy what remained of Fort Sunstrike's broken defenses, and even if they disobeyed their general and fired on the two sneering monsters before them, President Novak was as good as dead.

"We don't have to be afraid of you, and I refuse to hide from you any longer. Kill me if you want to, but you'll never break the Meridial spirit," the president declared, and puffed his chest out.

"You ridiculous little man, have you truly misread the situation so? Your man here is wise enough to be a demon, a pity he was born into your feeble nation. You only live to make Merryland's transition into a vassal state of the Apollyonic Empire smoother," Gall said.

"I will sign nothing. Torture me before your Emperor, pump one of your little demons into my body, but I will never, ever cede control of our ancestral, angel-granted lands to you wicked things," the president said, his chest heaving with emotion. He looked to General Gunn, but the old man had his eye turned downwards.

"I would rather just behead you here and now," Shatter said coldly, his arm shifting into its sword-mode. "But my orders are to end this war with as little bloodshed as is necessary. What sort of man are you, I wonder? Will you grandstand in hopes of becoming a statue after a century of bloodshed and suffering by your people? Or will you come with us, and sign our surrender, giving this ancient nation a chance to survive? I promise you; we can inflict so much more harm than we have, and I want so badly to massacre everyone in this room to avenge the suffering of my brothers," Shatter said.

"War is a game no one wins, not in the long run, kid," General Gunn said. "We fought to defend ourselves, but fathers who return home after gunning down enemies, after losing buddies, they're never the same. You'll carry the day, but the atrocities you've committed on our soil will never wash out. They will rot your withered souls, even wasted by centuries of evil as they are. Remember my words as you follow whatever your superiors order you to do next," the general said, and Gall began to laugh, the sound like a theremin warbling erratically.

"Bruce, you can't just throw down your gun like that," President Novak cried.

"Who said anything about throwing down my gun?" the old man said.

"Yes, do it! All good generals should inspire their men," Gall cried. Soldiers were moving down the hallway, breaking down doors as they went, cleaning up the last dregs of resistance that mattered.

The general removed his sidearm from his gun belt. Cocking the hammer, he put the gun against his temple, never taking his eye from Shatter. The chiropteran shuddered as Gall tittered happily, drinking in the dismay and horror of every human in the room as they gasped and started in their places.

The gunshot was like a cork popping out of a wine battle after all of the deafening gunfire that had torn through the air of the fortress. The general's dead body hitting the ground was the final gong before a human sacrifice.

"Lay down your weapons," Shatter said. The soldiers were silent. Some of them complied. One who was splattered with the general's gore stared through the demon as if he was a clear pane of glass, and he held his rifle as if it were a useless plank of wood. The war was over, and even President Novak could tell that his grandstanding was in vain. Between the sneering, psychic, insect demon and the cold, long-eared chiropteran, he no longer had any authority. The squad of demons that was drawing ever nearer just cemented Merryland's defeat.

"To whom will I tenure my surrender?" the President asked.

"That would be me," Admiral Warth said, marching through the open door at the head of his squad. "Is there a reason why some of you are still clutching your arms?"

The Meridial soldiers, defeated without firing a shot, looked somberly at the Ghoul Troopers who had their demonic weapons pointed at them. They saw, some of them for the first time, the barbarism and decadent body horror that belied the desperation of their enemy's struggle. The metal teeth beneath the skull-shaped helmets that were exposed whenever one licked his lips, the single glowing red eye that peered from a fiend's brutally scarred face, the swords and hooks that replaced hands and arms, the guns that were affixed to shoulders, the armor that was grafted to flesh. Shatter was practically untouched compared to some of the older Troopers, and the human soldiers who still held onto their rifles laid them on the ground at Warth's boots and raised their hands above their heads in submission. Warth stepped aside and addressed his men.

"Leave the three in the middle," he said, and turned his attention on the human soldiers. They recoiled as the demonic weapons came to life, their beams searing through their bodies as they burned them to their souls; the three who were still standing jumped as their comrades thumped on the ground, lifeless.

"Now we will go back the way we came. You'll address your people from the urchin, and the fighting will stop. I long for peace as much as you do," the admiral said, and motioned for President Novak to come to him. The man left the three remaining soldiers' side, careful to step over the dead men as he went towards the admiral. The Ghoul Troopers lowered their weapons, and Shatter stepped aside to let the president pass, his arm shifting back from its sword-mode. And then they heard the shouts and footfalls from deep within the fortress.

"I thought you had accounted for the husks here," Gall snarled at Warth, who glanced casually at the doorway.

"Why are you stopping? Your little friends won't get here soon enough to intercept us," the admiral said to the president. "You lot, get out there and tear them to shreds. Captain, Gall, you accompany me and the prisoners," he said, and turned on his heel, following in the wake of his Ghoul Troopers as they marched out of the control room.

"We're heading for the roof, my boys should hold the stragglers long enough for us to make our escape to Eggshank," Warth said as they briskly moved towards the staircase. He had a firm grip on President Novak's arm, and dragged the unfortunate man along with him while the three human prisoners followed closely, Shatter's Soul-Scorcher aimed at the back of their heads.

"It's not looking good, there's too many of them," Gall yelled at the back of Warth's head, tapping the side of his head.

"Why didn't you say something?" Warth asked irritably.

"I didn't hear their thoughts until they were a floor away! What do you think my range is?" Gall hollered back as an explosion bigger than any that had rocked the fortress up until then went off, rattling the walls and floor.

One of the human prisoners looked back, his eyes wide with hope, and Shatter prodded him with his Soul-Scorcher. They reached the stairs, but Warth stopped and whirled around.

"Execute these husks and slow those bastards down," he ordered Shatter and Gall, and turned to leave.

Shatter lifted his gun, scarcely registering what the admiral had just ordered.

"Not on your life, army slinger!" Gall declared, and drew his sword. Warth didn't slow as he ran up the stairs, gripping the President by the arm, but this proved to be a fatal mistake. The approaching human soldiers, though surging up the staircase on the other side of the building, had split their forces, and had a company coming up on that side as well. A soldier in the front leveled his rocket launcher at Shatter, but another soldier, on seeing the three terrified prisoners, grabbed him by the shoulder. He cursed as his missile went wide, striking the stairs above, raining rubble on the soldiers below.

Warth fell as the stairs below him exploded, leaving President Novak standing atop a staircase leading nowhere. Shatter ran for the president, while Gall stood his ground, watching as the soldiers reorganized themselves, surrounding Admiral Warth as they tried to come to terms with what their situation was. One of them shot the demon in the head, and the rest began to move again.

"Move, husk," Shatter growled, aiming his gun at the president.

Gall pulled a blaster from his belt and swiftly shot all three human prisoners in the head and ran from the landing as their lifeless bodies fell down the steps, flopping and thumping at the feet of the other soldiers. The others fired after the fleeing knight, missing sight of Shatter as they ran after him. The demon kept his Soul-Scorcher pressed against the president's heart, glaring into the shorter man's blue eyes with his empty demon eyes.

When the last of the human soldiers had passed them by, Shatter grabbed the president by his shirt and hurled him down the stairs as hard as he could. The small man hit the concrete with a harsh crack, and lay there moaning. Satisfied, Shatter shouldered his gun and spread his wings. Dropping swiftly down to where the admiral lay, Shatter retrieved the sky urchin's mobile console from the admiral's belt and ran back up the stairs.

"You'd best get up," Shatter said softly to the president.

"You broke my leg," the man sniffed, and Shatter sighed, listening to the sound of the human soldiers hunting Sir Gall.

"If you don't get up and fucking walk this second, I'm going to bite your ugly face off," Shatter said calmly.

The president shuddered, but he slowly got up. He wobbled on his right leg, yelling in agony, but there was no one to pay attention to him over the gunfire and screaming.

"Now move, down those stairs," Shatter said, and aimed the Soul-Scorcher at the man once more.

"That's Asdeev! Is Markus really dead?" the President asked as he complied, looking wistfully past the demon as he went down the stairs.

"The black-winged angel kid? I took this fine, angry mace off him before he fell out of the sky," Shatter replied, lightly touching the mace as it wobbled in its makeshift holster. The President was silent as he was directed to the floor below. They waited on the landing until the fighting had moved to the floor above, and emerged, moving towards the other staircase.

Shatter and the President made it to the room where he and Gall had entered the fortress, and the President could only look up, dumbfounded as Shatter operated the mobile console for the sky urchin.

"How did it all come to this?" the man asked no one as the bottom of the spinning sky urchin spiraled open and the indigo light of the tractor beam hummed to life, sweeping he and the demon up in it, as well as a discordant trail of rubble and smashed artillery.

Chapter 5: The Big Chair

President Jerome Novak, despite being a coward and largely without talent, regardless of what his political backers and speech writers would have his constituents think, was nonetheless not a stupid man. The young demon captain had thrown him into what passed for a brig aboard the alien vessel, a caged off segment of the lower compartment, where the enemy soldiers had been stationed. Novak sat quietly, eyeing the weaponry that was casually stored around the compartment. There were straps hanging from the ceiling, which the Ghoul Troopers would grip while they awaited deployment. Soul-Scorchers, swords, and other weapons were strewn across the floor, but Novak didn't kid himself with attempts at reaching them. He hadn't studied the intel on downed demonic sky urchins or their specialized weaponry, but he knew that their armature wouldn't work for him. Humans didn't have demonic souls, which were apparently more caustic and filled with energy than whatever humans were packing. Novak didn't know much about magic, but he knew that demons were capable of feats that humans could only dream of. In ancient times, before the Angelic Betrayal and Apollyon's opening of the Void, humans would summon demonic souls from the depths of the void to perform tasks and magical workings for them. That being the case, a Soul-Scorcher would do nothing if Novak pulled its trigger, except maybe send his body into shock from the feedback as it attempted to draw from his feeble human spiritual essence, and as for drawing one of the swords, Novak almost laughed out loud at himself, imagining trying to put his pudgy body into a fighting stance...

Instead, the President of Merryland busied himself by peering through the slats in the ceiling at the control hub of the sky urchin, where the young captain had taken his place in the command seat. There were chairs all around the sky urchin, with monitors and workstations that each sported different buttons and displays, and in the center, the chair where the Admiral had doubtlessly sat. Novak couldn't see from his vantage point, but by the way the captain was pushing down on the armrests of the seat, there were clearly buttons there, with which he was attempting to gain control of the vessel. It was clearly intended to be piloted by a crew, but the entirety of its crew was down below, slaughtering and being slaughtered in the fortress.

"I repeat, this is Ghoulking eight-nine-nine, anyone who hears me, respond, over," the captain was saying, looking from one monitor to another. There were monitors positioned all around the chair, and he swiveled around and around, glancing at different ones as he tried to make contact with other demons. The vessel's two horizontal halves rotated in opposite directions, humming as they made it defy gravity while providing a consistent gravitational field within the cabin.

"Fiend oh-three-six, if you can hear me, please respond, over," the captain said, the slightest hint of desperation in the young demon's voice.

Novak wondered if anyone knew where he was, or if there was any chance he would survive the crash when this sky urchin was inevitably shot down. He had been assured by both of his dead generals that the demons had pulled most of their flying machines out of Merryland, going home to Demon Land to quell some sudden civil disturbance in their megacity, Duskrim. They had taken him prisoner, but just barely.

"Fuck, there's no one out there," the young captain said to himself, hitting a series of buttons on his armrests. He climbed out of the seat and ran around the control hub, his boots thudding against the metal above Novak's head. The demon was looking at the other monitors at the other workstations, and was discovering what Novak had guessed, which was simply that the monitors around the big chair showed the readouts that were already displayed at the crews' workstations.

"Damn it, I've done everything I was supposed to do and more, what the fuck do I do now?" the captain said, a little more desperately. Novak was sure that if the sassy psychic knight with the bug-eyes and chainsaw-mouth had been in the captain's position, he would be even more useless. At least the captain had the good sense not to try to fly the demonic vessel without the proper know-how. The thuggish knight would have tried to fly his new trophy across the sea home to Demon Land himself, ending his and Novak's life right then and there.

The realities of command, it seemed to the president, were for first time since he was elected, defined as never before. Signing legislation and playing his part on TV, shaking hands with other Volusiapian heads of state, taking credit for trade deals and whatever reforms managed to get past the senate, while always threatening unilateral action against the endless saber-rattling of the demon scum were just the front-side of the job. He now saw clearly all his missed opportunities as the two generals, the nationalist fool, Dobbs, and the grizzled old hawk, Gunn, each scrambled over each other and asserted their vision of how things needed to be done, worried only about their own legacy. What would Novak have done, had the generals not been there to assure him they had everything under control? Would the fortress have fallen the same way, or even worse? Or could he have stopped Dobbs from destroying the cannons' tunnel system?

Up above, the captain, who had started this operation as a lieutenant, if Gunn was to be believed, was grappling with the same dilemma. The giant heads that had been telling him what to do were gone now, and it was up to him to seize control. The President of Merryland lay on his back and took a deep breath. His joints ached worse than his sprained ankle, and he knew that there was nothing left for him to do but wait for salvation or death, the same as the demonic captain above him. The only question now was which side Fate's penny would land on.

"*bzzt*...speaking...still alive, respond, over," a voice said over the speakers above the big chair.

Shatter ran back to the big chair, breathing heavily.

"Come in Fiend, this is Ghoulking reading you loud and clear," Shatter cried, his mechanical heart beating like a hammer against the inside of his chest.

Vermin's voice crackled through the static, still recognizable despite the disruption.

"...taking heavy fire, sir, husks are leaving their cannons to hunt that angel you dropped, we've been sighted and are hunkering...," Vermin said, and was abruptly cut off.

"Fuckers," Shatter swore, swiveling around to study the monitors around him. Most of them were hooked up to the other workstations, displaying their readouts, but they were designed to be redirected to other sources, displaying newscasts, video conferences, or weapon systems as the commander required. One of the five monitors was displaying the sky urchin's position on a digital map, while another was hooked into the radio system, displaying the frequency he was connected to. A third was offline, while the other two were connected to the navigation and weapons systems, and Shatter was uncomfortable with having to pilot the ship on his own. However, his men were out there, on the battlefield, and he was in control of the last sky urchin in Merryland, as far as he knew.

"So, it's true then, you really did kill Markus?" the president called meekly up to Shatter, shocking the demon as he considered his next course of action.

"Quiet, husk. You live at my mercy," the demon said, studying the buttons on his armrests.

"The cannons don't know you have me onboard, if you try to fly out of here, you'll get us both killed," the president said, hopeful that the demon couldn't do anything to him.

"Didn't you hear me? The cannon husks are abandoning their posts to find your little angel-boy," Shatter replied, and then looked up. A full flight panel was hanging above him. He puzzled over the buttons on his armrests, wondering how to make the flight array come down to him, and glanced over at the navigation station, wondering if he would need to just move there.

"Hey, I know you're all alone now, but if you surrender me to the soldiers down below, I will personally intercede on your behalf. As President of Merryland, I have the authority to pardon you," the president pressed.

Shatter stood up and grabbed the flight panel, and he sighed in relief as it came down easily, the trellis system it was joined to opening with little pressure.

"Okay, I can do this," Shatter muttered as he studied the controls on the flight array. He thought of Blusterfew, crushed under the rubble of the cannon as he desperately tried to take one more shot at their hated foes.

Vermin and Sarrow hunched beneath the burned metal shell that had been their stolen truck, wincing as bullets went through the steel, barely missing them as they took what refuge they could.

"Is he coming?" Sarrow yelled as the gunshots stopped. Sarrow bit the needle out of one of his last grenades and chucked it over the truck, wincing as it went off with a bang that hurled earth through the devastated truck at them.

"He's figured out how to fly the urchin, but he says he's sorry if he makes us puke because he has no idea how to fly," Vermin said.

"That's funny, he was a real ace against that fledgling," Sarrow replied, peering through one of the bullet holes. "Our friends are getting closer," he said to Vermin.

THE CANNONS OF MERRYLAND

Markus lay where he had fallen; the agony in his broken legs and his twisted spine was more than he could comprehend. One of his eyes was filled with blood, and his vision was clouded by veering stars and a red mist that colored everything in the hues of death as his eyesight failed, giving way to the relentless power of the night.

He wondered why there were no more cannonballs flying overhead. He drifted in and out of consciousness, imagining soldiers being herded out of their cannon stations, Soul-Scorchers pointed at their backs as demons laughed and yelled up at the starless sky. Evil had triumphed, evil had damaged one of his lush, beloved black wings, and now he would lay amongst the wreckage and desolation of war as evil marched to raze the walls he had so valiantly defended, just another wasted, broken weapon on this lost battlefield.

He heard the distant humming of the sky urchin he had come so close to striking from the sky, and it took all the strength he could muster to move his head to follow its progress as it spun through the dusty sky, hurtling towards the ruins of a destroyed cannon.

He knew in his gut that that cannon was the crack in Fort Sunstrike's armor. That cannon was the one the demons had taken, it was the cannon the other cannons had fired on, too late; and it was the one that his flesh-winged foe had issued from. With his one good eye he saw the final heartbreak of the day as the sky urchin powered on its tractor beam and the unmistakable shapes of three Ghoul Troopers ascended through the light-blue beam from the twisted metal and amorphous mounds of dirt of the battlefield. There was a limp, hulking form, a wiry humanoid demon, and a horned fiend. As his agony subtly overwhelmed his consciousness he wondered where the bat-winged fiend that had stolen Asdeev, his mace, from his hands, who had stolen the sky from him, was. Was he onboard the sky urchin, rapturing his friends away from the battlefield, or was he storming the hallways of Fort Sunstrike, murdering Meridial soldiers with Asdeev in his filthy claws?

The world spun away. Darkness filled the fledgling's mind. Through the shadows he felt himself lifted up off the ground where he lay like carrion, his broken legs dangling like an unstrung marionette's limbs. Rough hands carried him, a face with a beard like a tangled bush made of black smoke peered at him, his bleary eyes forced open by cold forceps as critical, alien eyes studied him. Voices like distant, muffled rainfall drifted hazily into his ears, and he faded away, unable to care or comprehend anything whatsoever, within him or outside. He was finished. Once he opened his eyes to see the blurred outline of Tolbert and Maria standing beside him, but they were ghosts conjured by his damaged mind. The dim lights flickered and he was gone again, lost in oblivion, even his dreams nothing but a lightless vacuum devoid of memory or feeling.

Shatter sat beside Gall in the command room of Fort Sunstrike, a few other demons from the late Admiral Warth's company present as well as the transmission came on the large Astitution Table in the center of the room. All of the demonic soldiers present still wore their blood-soaked outfits, having gotten no chance to change or relax.

"Are they transmitting?" one of the other demons said, looking around at the other surly faces that didn't bother to meet his eyes. Shatter didn't know the rank of the other demons, nor did he care at all. With Warth dead, Shatter assumed Sir Gall had taken charge of the battle, but that wasn't his concern. His squad, the Corrupters, were being treated in the infirmary of the fortress with the other casualties. Trex was in a catatonic state, and Shatter wondered what would become of his hatchlings. Sarrow's burns were being treated, as was Vermin's hand, but without demonic healers and a team of soul-crafters, there was little that could be done for them. They all needed to be flown back to Duskrim; with only one sky urchin at Fort Sunstrike and a small handful still stationed at the Dragon's Keep, it was doubtful that anyone would be flying home without a transport directly from Demon Land after how costly the war had been for the empire. They would not leave their prize unoccupied, not after so many deaths and so much hardware lost. It would be a disastrous spiral that no amount of propaganda would be to pull the senatorial administration out of if they lost Merryland after capturing the president. Why so much of the hardware and manpower had been abruptly pulled back over the ocean was a staggering mystery, but here they were, about to be addressed by another general. Another old, self-assured monster in a suit with a sash full of medals ready to tell them where their next meat grinder would be. Shatter sighed, imagining Vermin's rustic parents when the young fiend went home. What would his sacrifice mean to them when he couldn't push a rake or milk a cow?

You moron, he's going to get a bionic hand, just like you, Shatter reminded himself irritably, looking ruefully down at his weaponized hand.

The projection on the Astitution Table finally came to life, and Shatter practically jumped in his chair. His father, Senator Malekarm, stood on the steps of the Senatorial Palace. He wore his typical expensive suit, his wings draped over his shoulders like a leather cape.

"Good evening, proud soldiers of Apollyon. I am told that the end of the war is nigh?" the senator said, a forced smile on his haggard face. The demons in the room stirred, looking at one another, and out of the corner of his eye, Shatter saw Gall open his mouth to speak, but Shatter stood up.

"I have the President of Merryland imprisoned aboard our one sky urchin. He's going nowhere. We're in the process of taking over the cannons. Our Ghoul Troopers are organized here, at the fortress, where our banners fly," Shatter said.

Malekarm looked like he was about to orgasm right there in his pants.

"My son, I was told that you're a captain now! I regret to…" Malekarm started to say, but Shatter cut him off.

"Why did you feeble paper-crinklers leave us out here to die?" Shatter said, trembling with rage.

"We did no such thing," Malekarm said, his enthusiasm not dulled one bit.

"My boys are hurt, we nearly lost our lives taking that cannon, and Bluster is dead. Where did our sky urchins go?"

"There was a national emergency, boy. Move the watcher orb, let him see what remains of Washer's Square," Malekarm said, and the camera that was trained on the senator swiveled around to show the regal forum where the Senatorial Palace was built. The proud statues of demonic heroes and lords were no more, lost amongst the rubble of downed sky urchins and busted pavement. A sewer pipe was spewing filthy water into the air like a parody of a fountain, and Ghoul Troopers were digging through the ruins, scanning for survivors.

"Hear the sirens? Hear the terrified mothers? Hear the burning factories? If not for your brother, Splinter, we would have lost everything this day. The plight of your comrades is not an abstraction for me, Captain," Malekarm said as the camera spun back to him. "However, the lives of our citizens, human and demon alike, were in direct peril this day. That is why, despite the concerns of our invasion being secondary, your valiant actions this day are legendary. You demons won us the country of Merryland, a territory we have been striving to conquer for centuries. We now have a foothold in the continent of Volusiapia, and more land for our farmers and less privileged to settle."

"What happened, Senator?" Gall asked, his wings twitching nervously.

"The details are still fuzzy, but you will learn all when you come home. On behalf of the entire Senate and the rest of the Empire, I am here to thank you for your service and assure you that backup is coming," the senator said.

"I got a question," one of the other demons said. "Why are you talking to us? Where's General Asterious and Storm?"

"They're on their way back to Merryland. As I said, your backup is inbound," Malekarm said, his eyes glittering. He was no longer looking so happy.

"You pulled them away from the Dragon's Keep?" Shatter asked, feeling like his head was going to explode.

"The Over-Seer invoked the Implosion Directive. We would have pulled Warth as well, but he insisted on keeping the pressure up on your theater. He's lucky his gamble paid off and the president was actually there," Malekarm replied.

"Warth is dead," one of the other demons said, and held up the admiral's sash as proof.

Malekarm was silent. The transmission abruptly ended, leaving the exhausted group of frustrated, confused demons watching the empty space above the table where the projection had been.

Shatter left the room as the other demons erupted in rage, arguing over what would happen next. There were probably countless openings in the top brass now, and they were all war heroes now. Who would get to sit behind the captured president as he gave his surrender speech? Who would get to execute him? Who would be the governor of this new land? Think of all the Meridial women ripe for the taking! Shatter walked out without slamming the door as the other demons rubbed their scaly claws together and groused over the future. He was disgusted, and wanted nothing more than to get out of his filthy, smelly uniform and shower. He knew Gall had followed him out of the command room, but he wasn't turning around to talk to the showboating knight.

Had his father noticed the great mace in his hands? Would his horrible deeds this day matter to his ambitious father beyond what it would mean to his political aspirations? As he undressed, leaving his filthy fatigues on the barracks floor, he looked down darkly at his bionic arm. He missed the feeling of touching things with his fingertips. He remembered his warm, scaly arm, remembered the slender bones that would dance up his arm when he moved his fingers. The hot water washed the blood and grime of the past two months off his body, but under the celebrations of the soldiers on the floors above, under the droning of the doomed president's speech of surrender, under the hissing of the hot showerhead, Shatter's sensitive bat ears could hear the mechanical whirring of his bionic heart, thumping as it pumped his blood through his body, still safe within his own veins for the time being.

Thank you so much for reading "The Cannons of Merryland"! Giving Shatter, Splinter's nastier older brother was something I was really looking forward to, especially after his brief, violent role in *The Struggle*. Now that poor Void is gone, Shatter is Splinter's only sibling left now (or is he?), and I have grand plans for Shatter and his battle-torn Ghoul Troopers. If you enjoyed this hellish trek through the closing moments of Demon Land's campaign for Merryland, please visit the official Demon Land Books Facebook page, where I write about books, movies, and different things going on in the fantasy world, as well as announcements for future books set on or around Erde. Also be sure to check out Demonlandbooks.com, and definitely don't miss my email list, where I send my subscribers exclusive content!

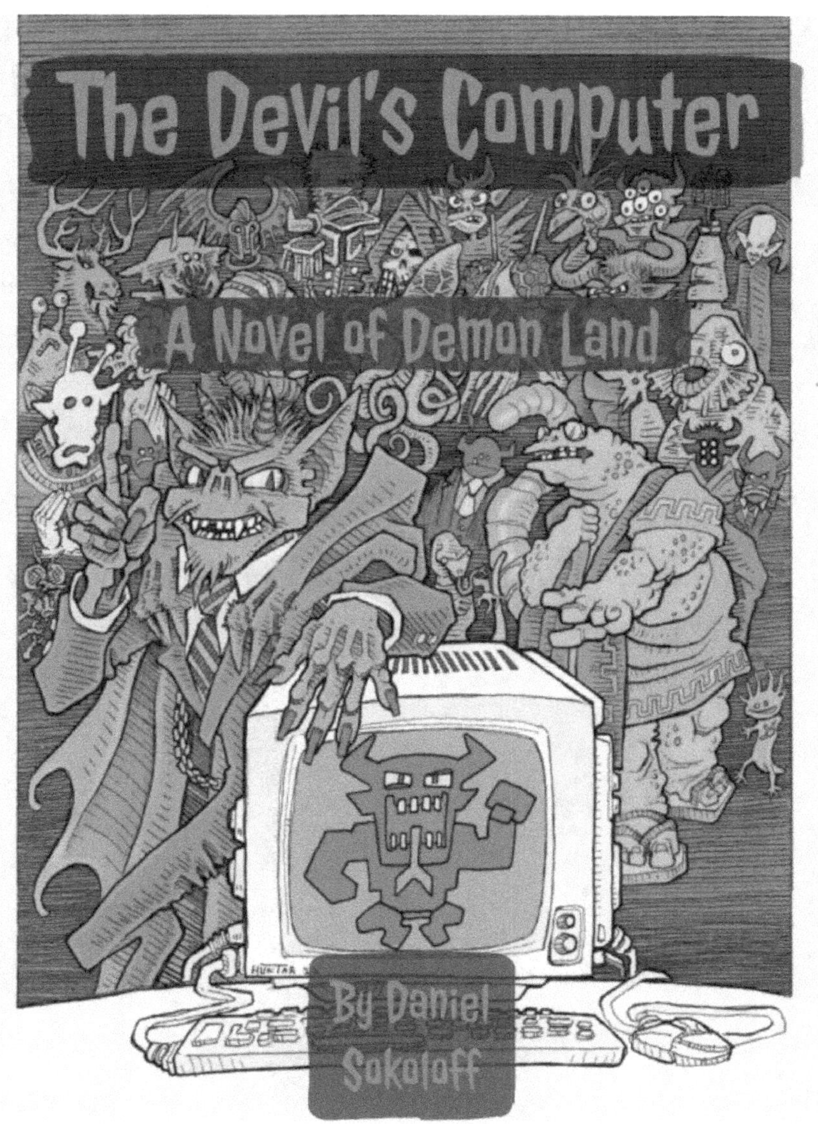

The Devil's Computer
A Novel of Demon Land
By Daniel Sokoloff

THE CANNONS OF MERRYLAND

Don't miss the next chapter in the ongoing saga of Demon Land! "The Devil's Computer" stars Splinter's ruthlessly ambitious father, Senator Malekarm, as he plots to fill the power vacuum in the Empire of Apollyon. As human terrorist attacks rock the empire and the balance of power shifts with the long-sleeping Emperor gone, Malekarm comes across a plot to build a computer with the mind of Great Satan recreated within it. What's a power-hungry demon to do, except try to use this to his advantage? The computer has a mind of its own though, and it's own ambitions probably don't align with Malekarm's blood-sucking ethos. To make matters worse, his illegitimate daughter is involved in more ways than one. I wonder, what does Splinter think of all this? After the thunderous cannons of Merryland, this is next story that will determine the trajectory of all souls on Erde, human and demon alike! Features a cover design by none other than Hunter Jackson, also known as Techno Destructo!

Don't miss out!

Visit the website below and you can sign up to receive emails whenever Daniel Sokoloff publishes a new book. There's no charge and no obligation.

https://books2read.com/r/B-A-JYXV-PAMGC

BOOKS2READ

Connecting independent readers to independent writers.

Also by Daniel Sokoloff

Demon Land
The Struggle
The Cannons of Merryland

Watch for more at https://lokepoet.weebly.com/.

About the Author

Daniel Sokoloff lives in Philadelphia, and grew up in Brooklyn, New York. His experiences growing up in cities informs the depiction of the demonic cities in his books. He also moonlights as a poet and occultist, dabbling in demonolatry and divination. His first book of poetry, *Dream of the Ash*, is about his relationship with the god of wisdom, Odin.

Read more at https://lokepoet.weebly.com/.